D1357948

ALSO BY DAVID BAJO

The 351 Books of Irma Arcuri
Panopticon
Mercy 6

The Ensenada Public Library

A Novel by

David Bajo

BRIGHT
HORSE
BOOKS

Printed in the United States of America

Brighthorse Books
13202 N River Drive
Omaha, NE 68112
brighthorsebooks.com

ISBN: 978-1-944467-11-1

Brighthorse books are distributed to the trade through Ingram Book Group and its distribution partners. For more information, go to https://ipage.ingramcontent.com/ipage/li001.jsp. For information about Brighthorse Books, go to brighthorsebooks.com. For information about the Brighthorse Prize, go to https://brighthorsebooks.submittable.com/submit.

For Elise

“I have always imagined that Paradise will be a kind of library.”

—Jorge Luis Borges

One

THE NEXT TIME YOU stand in the stacks, look to that space left by a borrowed book. Note the shape. Is it sharp and clean, rectangular because the books on either side of it remained perfectly in place after the pull? If your library is any good, that will be the case. If you're in my library, that will be the case. Put your nose to it. That fossil scent, ink and paper sewn together for decades, maybe centuries, will instantly sharpen your intelligence, your awareness, your understanding of time and life and what is to be treasured.

Peer into the darkness. It will look like a grand hallway taking you to some ancient place of learning and shared wisdom, and it will be empty and not so inviting because the far end is dark and mysterious, light and shadows falling from unseen corners. You could easily imagine the echo of footsteps in there.

If you dare, if you have been a regular, without touching the book on either side, slide your hand into the space. Close your eyes, recall the scent, and you might feel the compression of all the other books, those that remain, those many more that have passed. I don't know what that compression is. History? Technology? Whim? A mix of those three? Maybe I don't know anymore because I am a librarian and no longer a pure and true reader. Maybe, uncorrupted, you will feel it right away and know.

I miss reading, the way it used to be for me, before I became a curator and steward of books. The irony is crushing. Maybe that is the compression I feel whenever I slide my hand into that space. To you, a library is a place where books are saved and celebrated, a Valhalla of sorts. To me, a library is a place of reckoning.

And that space, that clean rectangular gap between books, is not always what you think. You probably see it and think someone has borrowed a book, maybe taken it home for a month or just for an hour or two to pass some time in the quietly lit reading room. But the book that was once there might be lost or stolen or destroyed. We call them *stolens* because a book that is borrowed and not returned, a book that is borrowed and forgotten, a book that is borrowed and not cared for enough to keep from ruin, is a stolen book.

All those other books on either side of that gap and all those filling the stacks appear even more still because they don't shift after a book is removed. They don't collapse over and toward one another and the gap is preserved as space for return. But all of those books are not as still as they appear. To me they are a forever-shifting mass, a glacier of paper pushing with imperceptible yet strong and constant force. I feel it whenever I'm in the stacks. It's similar to the press you may feel whenever you wander among large boulders or sequoias, a thumb on your temples, your shoulders, your heart.

For books are forever coming into a library—new releases, new editions, replacements for damaged, over-used classics. In the US last year, 304,912 new releases and re-editions were published. The New York City Public Library holds fifty-three million books with an annual circulation of thirty-five million. I do not work there. I work at the Ensenada Public Library which holds 1.2 million books and has an annual circulation of 3.3 million.

It's more like a lava flow than a glacier, in that it's faster and just as relentless, with an underlying sense of urgency if you choose to step into its path. Of course, it's my job to step into its path. We here at the EPL want you to be able to stand among the stacks and sense that quivering stillness of collective knowledge and imagination. We don't want you to know you are standing in a lava flow. We keep our shelves tight. When you remove a book, the remaining gap will be crisp, dark and perfectly rectangular.

Two

I WAS PADDLING THE morning glass just behind the break when the first book bobbed past the nose of my board. As though drowned, the book floated face-down, spread open above the depths. Salt and water damage obscured the title and author but I could make out the silvery Dewey Decimal number: 516.3, a volume on analytic geometries. When I reached for it, my fingers passed through the underbelly of pages, the paper dissolving easily as sea foam. The remnants were then sucked up the back of a swell and hurled into the mighty break. Nothing could have vanished more completely.

A surfer shot along the top of the curl, oblivious, wetsuited head to toe, his dark form slick and crouched above the water before he dropped into the wave. I imagined his tailfins slicing through the pulpy remains of 516.3. The late winter swell, too challenging for the likes of me, had drawn the best riders this morning.

The second book bumped my seaward side. 635.1, making it a volume on edible roots. This one I caressed onto my board, my gentle hand only touching the hardcover and spine. I pressed the volume as closed as possible and centered it on the nose of my board. I had to eye the swells coming in on my right while making sure to stay clear of the powerful suck to my left. I could sense the wary eyes of the surfers in the lineup behind me. They knew me. They knew I would try to stay clear and just paddle. But the break this morning was big and glassy with perfect shape. And I was messing with these books, distracted.

A line of three volumes was drifting toward me. I gathered

them all and stacked them in twos. They stuck nicely in the lumpy wax. But that left me with a problem. Without the books, I was just going to belly-ride my way to shore on an unwanted roller, let my board shoot out from under. With the books, I would have to paddle several hundred yards to get around the point, clear of the big break. Wearing just a thin spring suit, I was already cold.

One of the surfers broke from the lineup and approached. Orange dreads gathered like flax, long body, powerful strokes, a nose as sharp as his board, it was Flaco. Flaco was a local, as good as any of the pros who came down from Redondo and Manhattan to practice away from the crowds and amateurs. Flaco had no taste for contests and trophies. And sometimes he checked books from the library, usually stuff on gardening.

"Part of me just wants to watch." He drew next to me. "You'd wipeout without those books on your nose. With them, you get creamed. We'll be unwrapping you from the kelp."

"But part of you," I said, "wants to see if you're good enough to ride them in yourself, clean, without losing a one."

"I'm the only one with a chance." He looked back toward the lineup. "Maybe Villaran. But he doesn't care for books. Besides, I haven't ridden a longboard in years."

•

FLACO LET ME GO in first while he waited for the next good set. His board was too much for me, quicksilver under my belly. I never once considered popping into a stance as I took the first unwanted and unclaimed wave. I slid down the face, holding on like a little boy on a sled, the curl thundering alongside, hitting me with a jet of salt spray. I fought to keep the nose clear. I had to open the library in less than an hour.

There wasn't much beach for this pointbreak, not even

during the lowest tide. Like a lot of the little surf havens along the Baja coast, this one was just a grotto in the black cliffs. You had to park a hundred yards away, walk your board along the narrow highway, then find the first gap at the cliff-top, a tricky eight-foot jump, board in hand. This began a series of hops and rocky trails down to a wedge of sand you couldn't see until the last jump. For the return climb, there was a rope at the top. Most surfers had to toss their boards up, then climb that last eight feet. Experts like Flaco could haul their boards with them. Flaco maintained the rope and knocked down any cairns amateurs would stack to mark the spot. When the tide came in, it all disappeared. They called it and themselves Brigadoons.

I was alone on the cusp of sand. I sat on Flaco's board and watched the lineup. Out of the cold water, I heated up fast in my suit. I let it get uncomfortable, then unzipped to feel that fresh vulnerability, the first peel of an orange, better than any morning coffee.

I tasted the salt on my lips, felt it dry and tighten along my neck and torso. I'd wait till my lunch break to shower in the library basement. I loved the ocean on my skin, the scent of kelp and brine. My ex told me it kept me looking young, but I never knew if she was joking.

Flaco, with my longboard stacked with four books on its nose, stood out in the lineup. Tall for a surfer, a mean dark blade above the water, he always stood out in the lineup. But out there in those big perfect sets, with those books and that unwieldy board, his orange dreads tumbling loose from their bundle, he stood out in a different way. I thought of a clown about to ride a tricycle across a tightrope. The next wave was his to claim.

Old for such a great rider, still he was ten years younger

than I. The younger Brigadoons idealized him as their future, believing if they just kept at it, lived like they lived, that they would always be able to climb these cliffs up and down and shoot the mammoth curls of these winter swells year after year. But even the trophy winners like Villaran were wrong to believe that. There has to be something special about you, something deep and unique, something valuable, to survive the circulation.

I didn't know much about Flaco. I was afraid of learning how he made money. Because I checked out his borrows at the library, I knew his real name was Emilio Mendes-Kohl and that he was a resident of Ensenada. I knew he believed that there was only one big life that we all shared and participated in until death. To him, there was no such thing as "my life" or "your life" or anyone's "life path." Or "taking one's life."

"Picture it as a terrarium," he explained to me once as I scanned for him a book on subtropical fruits. "One that expands and contracts according to where you find yourself. Sometimes it's just a room, sometimes it's a whole park or a beach that extends to the horizon. Everyone's in it, living in it, doing their stuff. One thing, one time, one big single life going on, with hermit crabs and presidents."

Those in the lineup always played it cool when another claimed a wave, pretending not to care about the drop and ride, feigning interest in the incoming swells or a blemish in their wax, side-glances only. But now most of them were openly turned to watching Flaco with the books and longboard as he dug his arms hard in the water to get ahead of the break. I knew he wouldn't take a sensible ride. I knew he would wait for the best and biggest in the set, as though nothing were different, as though he had his razor board and no cargo.

When he popped into his stance, I could hear the shouts from the lineup. With the lumbering board, he could do nothing fancy. He rode with elegance, like the ancient big wave riders used to surf, driving along the face, legs planted. He looked like those statues of discus throwers. He thrust the nose forward, offering the books to the sea. If he had his board, he would have backed into the curl, let himself disappear into the white thunder, reappear miraculously at the end, standing and intact. He would have swung out, maybe spun in the air. But with his cargo and a board as long as a car, he fought to stay in front, to endure the snowy explosion behind him. Never had I seen books so delicately delivered.

•

ONSHORE, HE BROUGHT THEM to me. His breath was labored and his legs were strained, his lean muscles trembling beneath the wetsuit as he carried the stack across the deep sand. He placed the books on his board which I was still using for a seat. Hands on knees, he gathered his breath.

"Can you really repair these, Jack?" His lips remained parted, lungs pumping.

"Repair?" I pressed down on the stack, forcing water out. The books sighed. "These guys are beyond that. I just want to examine them. See whose they are, where they came from."

"They're not yours?"

"We don't dump books into the ocean. We record our overflow and store it in a Tijuana shipping annex. We incinerate our discards and damages."

Flaco dropped into a crouch. Water dripped from his dreads and chin. Sand clung to the stubble on his jaw, making it appear even grayer. "These look like yours."

I examined the spines. All of the decimals were hand-written in silver ink. It could have been Cisco's writing. He was the original head librarian at the EPL, dating back to the time before we imprinted the decimals. He still worked there even though he could never remember any of our names. The only thing he could really remember was our holdings. All of them, all titles and their numbers, from stacks to reference, our living card catalogue.

I pried open one of the top books. I had to use a shell to scrape the sodden pages away from the front plate. I tried to do it in a way that would not erase the stamp in the upper left-hand corner. Everything had turned to gum. Flaco reached to help. He knew I had a tremor. I pushed away his hand, gave him a look of caution, then raised a magician's finger.

I sprinkled some sand on the plate corner, then rubbed in gentle circles. The stamp—a ghost really—emerged. It was ours, the palm tree emblem undeniable.

"Did you see any more out there?" I asked, still looking at the EPL emblem.

"I thought I saw a line of them out past the swells. Coming in with the tide. But they might have been jellies." Flaco scanned the water. From behind us, the rising sun was hitting the swells. With it came the first morning zephyrs. The glass was vanishing. "But who would dump books into the ocean?"

He went to fetch my board. He had left it at the shore so he could carry the books to me. Beyond him I could see the lineup start to grab the last waves before the wind picked up. I tried spotting the line of books or jellyfish, but sunlight was shimmering on the ripples. When I eased my eyes toward the horizon, I caught sight of a gray whale. Just a nose and spout above the surface, then the bow of its great back, still it was grand. It was making its way south to Scammon's Lagoon, where it would breed. All the Pacific grays bred there and in a few other lagoons down the coast.

Baja was a land of many legends and myths, most of them small, most of them not very old and made up during the twentieth century by loony ex-pats. One I most wanted to be true was about the underwater passage undercutting the peninsula, used by the grays as a short cut to the Sea of Cortez. How else to explain how a few suddenly appeared on the other side, mated and relaxed in the calmer and warmer waters? Why else would they go to that narrow sea?

Three

In white shirt and black tie, I arrived. Salt prickled my skin and sand thickened my hair. I put on my nametag to help Cisco remember. As always, he was here first, sweeping the terra cotta walkways and stoop, a ritual he had performed every working day dating back decades, back to when he was the head librarian. He dowsed the terra cotta with a splash of water from his tin bucket, then swept vigorously with a straw broom. The rhythmic brushing always sounded somewhat festive, preparatory and welcoming. The air smelled of wet earth. Bougainvillea, almost always in bloom, lined the walkway leading to the white stucco library.

I could time myself according to Cisco's progress up the walkway. His fresh guayabera was always pressed and bright enough to reflect the scarlet of the bougainvillea. I was usually the first one to step across his work. His broom was my turnstile.

"Buenos, buenos." His big eyes lingered on my nametag—Jack Zajora, EPL Librarian. He looked like a bantamweight Picasso. "Buenos, Jackie Z."

The wonderful morning surf and the troubling line of drowned books had me in somewhat of a fugue. I wanted to kiss the top of his brown bald head.

"Buenos días, Cisco."

He wasn't Mexican. His full name was Francis Bellevue. He was from Battle Creek, Michigan, with a library science degree from Wayne State. He really did have a photographic memory and knew every book that had circulated through the library, every Dewey Decimal number, every reference title. Ten years ago, after we went fully digital, we incinerated the card catalogue. That was hard, shoveling those hundreds of thousands of cards into the fiery maw. Knowing Cisco had them in his head helped all of us quite a bit. Those cards were in the muscle memory of our fingers, their scent a patina on our breath.

That was a tough time for all of us. Other public libraries in the California system had elected to use the card catalogue destruction as a fundraising device. They sold them as bookmarks for one dollar a piece or ran contests where patrons had to use them as story prompts or as art objects. The L.A. and San Diego public libraries pressed us to do something similar. They always tried hard to use us as proving ground. But we elected to incinerate the cards. We needed the finality, a full sense of passage—out of the paper and into the digital.

It took us two days, all four librarians working in shifts, shoveling the cards into the fire. It helped that we had our own incinerator, just up the hillside, overlooking the harbor. Incinerators were allowed in Baja. For that alone, we were the envy of the California system. It was cheap and easy—and kind of fun and cathartic—for us to dispose of our rejects.

It was particularly tough for me then because my divorce from Marisa was taking shape at the same time. As I shoveled the cards, felt the wave of heat, heard the rush of flames, saw the white plume of smoke grow against the blue sky, I could not help but feel myself passing through as well.

Cisco brushed away my footprints.

I recited to him the Dewey Decimal of the first book I had tried to rescue this morning, the one on analytic geometry.

He kept sweeping. He pursed his lips.

"*Living in Cylinders: Unrolling Quadratic Surfaces.*" He paused and looked at me. "Mattison, R. 1986."

I raised my hand before he could tell me how many pages, who the publisher was. His Picasso eyes, almost sullen, all absorbing, held me. This was never a game with him. He was not our mascot. I had to give him my end, my reason.

"I found it in the ocean this morning," I told him. "I tried to save it but the surf was too big."

I said nothing about my clumsy attempt.

"Books in the sea," he replied. He resumed sweeping. "We do better tossing them to the flames."

•

I UNLOCKED THE FRONT doors. Heavy oak, each with a carving of our palm tree emblem, they swung true and quiet, welcoming all readers who would stroll the clean terra cotta walk, climb the sun-warmed stoop. I deactivated the alarm and then did what I always did when I opened the EPL, whenever I was the first one in. I cut across the foyer and stepped through the archway leading into the reading room.

For all of us EPL librarians, from Cisco to me, a library was only as good as its reading room. And ours was grand. It formed the vertical line of the T, thrusting out on its own from the three-storied front. It was a single room two stories high, with a skylight cupola and tall narrow windows. Books lined its walls and a catwalk traversed the second story shelves. Oak reading tables lined the entire floor, green desk lamps for each chair. Our model was the 42nd Street NYCPL reading room. And we fought for it. Los Angeles and San Diego constantly pressured us, haggled us about the space. They poured books into us and pointed at our reading room.

At the conferences in Sacramento, I always waited for the moment when the L.A. and San Diego people would exhibit the slide of our reading room, an image meant to punctuate our waste of space. Every time, the chapel-like image, lit by golden Baja sun, would have the opposite effect on the audience. I loved that particular hush. I made the yearly trek to Sacramento to hear it, to let it speak for me.

This morning, a swallow that had spent the night in the upper reaches darted overhead and made its way through the arch, across the foyer, and out the open doors. I clicked on a couple of the desk lamps, one on each side of the room, adding invite for the first morning readers.

I left the reading room and took my place at the front desk, a circle in the center of the foyer. Inside this circle, we had a sense of command. The pivot of a compass, it eased us toward all points that mattered most: the reading room, the two wings, and the entrance.

There were four of us. Catalina, our head librarian, took over ten years ago when Cisco decided it was best for him to step down. They would have offered it to me, but they were convinced I was about to accept a position at the new San Diego Public Library. In addition to Cisco and myself, there was a new hire, a Valeria Merced, who I had yet to meet, come down from the San Francisco Public Library.

It was odd that I hadn't met her, because all of us were usually directly involved in any hire. Merced was sent to us from Sacramento. Even Cat had yet to meet her. All we knew was that she was, in Sacramento's words, bringing us fresh ideas and that she would be arriving sometime this week. When Cisco first heard of this, he put a hand on my shoulder and said, "Don't forget. There's a difference between what is sent by request and what is just sent."

Cat told him not to worry.

Still holding my shoulder, but turning to her, he said, "I'm not the one who needs to worry."

Four

Cisco's brushstrokes made their way to the stoop. I closed my eyes and relaxed inside the circle, listening for the intermittent splashes from his bucket. I could tell when he reached the stoop. Each of the three steps received a splash, then three firm strokes. There was the click of tin, the rhythmic sweeps, repeated three times. Then on to the landing, which received the last big splash, then nine strokes delivered in sets of three. Often, I heard the song in my dreams, especially those I had napping on the beach, where the sound of the surf blended into the whisk of Cisco's broom.

There is another Baja legend that says if you stay here five years you stay here forever. I had been at the EPL for seven years when San Diego offered me the job. But it wasn't Baja that made me stay. I really felt that, as a librarian, I could do more here. Marisa disagreed. She left, in part I think, to show me that the legend bore no truth.

She returned—to Baja, not to me—two years later. She married a chef in Los Angeles and they moved just up the coast from Ensenada to take over Calafia, the best place to drink margaritas, eat lobster, and watch the gray whale migration. Marisa managed the place while Jimbo cooked. He made the real kind of margarita, served clear and on the rocks and tasting like the ocean. Enough of those and you spotted whales whether they were there or not.

Cisco brought his broom and bucket inside, stored them, and pinned his nametag to his guayabera. He waved to me before he began pushing one of the carts loaded for re-stacking. I looked up *Living in Cylinders*. We had filed it for outside storage. For space reasons, we had to send books that hadn't been touched for ten years into those Tijuana shipping bins. We put a lot of work into this process. For instance, if a book is removed from the shelf and then left on a reading table, that counts as a touch. That's one reason why you'll see those signs that ask you to please not restack books. Realize this. If you remove a book, read one sentence or look at one picture or one statistic, then slip it back, you deny that book its providence.

If someone wants to borrow a book in storage, we will retrieve it. It will take us three days to a week, but we will be happy to do it. We track that list carefully, monitor it every day. If there is just one book on the list, we contact that vast yard in Tijuana and find the title and bring it back to the EPL. It is a hard truth of libraries today. We have to outsource our dormant holdings.

It helps to have Cisco and his book memory. We feel a little better about sending books to Tijuana. We tell ourselves—we say it out loud to one another—that the dormant books are still active inside of him.

I had never read a book on analytical geometry. I had never considered how one would go about calculating the inside surface area of a cylindrical room. But now, after hearing that title, I had. If you ever feel the need to fire your imagination, just stand in a random stack and read the titles. Turn off your cell and go blank. The vertical torque itself will do something to your mind, release something.

At that moment, staring at the read-out for *Living in Cylinders*, I could do nothing but mourn for the title and hope that some library, anywhere in the world, still had it. I had no time to begin such a trace. That was leisure. I had work to do.

The first readers were coming in. Though they were counted

electronically at the door, I had to acknowledge them with a look, maybe a smile. And I had to assess our new arrivals. They came to us in cartons of one hundred. In the center of our circle desk were four cartons, one for each of us. Our goal was to get through at least one carton per day per librarian. This was one of the things we did in between checking in and checking out books, providing information over the counter, over the website, over the phone.

I broke open my carton. The night before, Cat had stamped our initials on our designated allotments. A book had one of two fates: reject or accept. The rejects were burned. The acceptances were registered, given their decimals, and stacked. Our acceptance rate was less than one in four hundred. Yes, of the four hundred titles with me inside the circle that day, 399 would be incinerated. The firemen in *Fahrenheit 451* had nothing on our ruthless selves.

The first book I lifted from my carton was a paperback, perfect binding, slick cover, some odd size outside of any known major or minor publishing house. Already its fate was shaky. It was titled, *Fly Away Home: A Father's Life as a Mother*. Inside the circle desk, we had a burn chute. One simply had to lift the flap, drop the book, and listen for the tiny pop at the end of its fall into the basement bin.

I checked for an ISBN, noted the publishing information on the copyright page, tested the gutter for quality of stock and binding. It smelled of store-bought cake. I chose a random sentence: "Those were the moments, I knew, those were the moments that would stick in my heart until its last beat."

Another reader entered. She was old, dressed as though coming from church, and carrying a stack of four returns. I smiled and thanked her as she slid the returns into the slot.

Without looking away from her, I lifted the burn flap and sent *Fly Away Home* down the chute. It made the sound of a single heartbeat, a one-two tumble into the depths. It was in my hands all of thirty seconds.

Five

By ten till noon, I had checked out 107 titles for twenty-five readers, carted all 227 returns for Cisco to re-stack, and plunged forty-three would-be books into the incinerator bin. The sand and salt from my morning swim no longer felt pleasant beneath my clothes. The invigorating prickle and tightness on my skin had warmed and softened. The fresh bristle of the ocean surface had turned to something bottom dwelling, a mollusk film. I was looking forward to my lunch time shower. But I had to wait for Cat to arrive.

Cisco and I could handle the usual weekday morning press. The art of the library is to appear cavernous, quiet, un-busy, while all the while taking care of the endless circulation of readers and titles, that relentless lava flow. I spun on my chair and peered through the archway. The reading room seemed scantly occupied. The noon sun cast it in a soft yellow, steeped with the softer green of the lamps. The only sound was that of the occasional page being flipped. From my angle I could see three readers scattered over two tables.

But without referring to the digital counter, I could tell more than forty readers were in there. We had forty tables, twenty per side, ten chairs per table. If solitary readers were already sharing tables, then we were now over forty. From the frequency of page flips, that crackle of adventure, I could gather we were somewhere over fifty.

Someone entered the library. I spun, closing the cover of my carton as I eased into the stop. The man was not a reader. Dressed in a silk shirt and gray fedora, he walked directly to the desk and knocked on it with the back of his knuckles.

He scanned the foyer, peered through the arch, adjusting his eyesight to the indoor light.

"I am confused," he said in Spanish. Cigar smoke lingered on his breath and clothes.

"You're looking for The Library," I said.

Eyeing the reference stacks in the foyer, he nodded.

"The place you're looking for is on Macheros. Near the taxi stand."

"Ah." He adjusted his fedora. "Sorry."

"No problem. We're here to serve."

We get ones like this about five times a day, though usually not this early. There are three main libraries in Ensenada: the EPL, La Biblioteca Municipal de Ensenada, and La Biblioteca. The latter is not a library. It is a high-end strip club. All three of us play an annual basketball tournament, three games to fifteen, whoever scores the most points total is that year's champion. We, along with La Biblioteca Municipal, tried for years to get the club to change its name. They argued that the name was too good for business. The basketball tournament was a kind of solution. The winner got to name the other two. But the club, with its bouncers, won every time. They were kind. They provided cheerleaders and refreshments and let us keep our names.

I looked at Cisco's carton. He had broken the seal and gone through about two dozen titles. When he didn't need to be inside the circle desk, he liked to take his allotment of new arrivals into the stacks and review them there. He claimed this gave him the best perspective.

Once, about three years ago, when we were together in the circle, I asked him if he had ever dumped books without looking at them. If he had ever looked at the clock, felt weary, and just sent the last titles at the bottom of his carton into the flames. I remember how the light was when I asked, a late afternoon slant with too much demand to it.

"No, Jack Zajora." He lifted one he was considering, held it between thumb and finger like a fish. "I'm often tempted. When I see one like this." Entitled *My Purgatory Years*, it was an autobiography of a former child television actor.

Cisco dropped it into the chute. "It's easy for us to think that the next one, the next seven, will be no better." He pulled another from his carton and held it up for both of us to consider.

"But see!" He tapped the cover. *Rotating Dreams: A History of the Viewmaster*. "Something different. If not better."

Yes, we—librarians, stewards of written knowledge, gatekeepers for the scribes—burn four hundred books per day. And those are the ones that make it through the digital rejections. But remember that publishers send us over 300,000 titles a year. And we know that number will keep growing because that is exactly what has happened ten years in a row. When I first started at the EPL seventeen years ago, the annual number had just reached 100,000. I remember how helpless that milestone made all of us feel.

The final morning breeze rustled the bougainvillea and blew through the front entrance. Noon warmth trailed softly behind. Cisco, on his way to another stacking cart, stopped to bask in this particular spill of air. He faced the entrance, opened his arms, and took a deep breath.

I sensed someone entering the circle, slipping behind me, no more sound than the closing of a book. It was Catalina. She had used the basement entrance. I continued to watch Cisco.

"Don't you wonder what he thinks about?" Cat asked, her voice at my shoulder, scented with peppermint and cigarette.

"I think if anyone really got into someone else's mind, into their thoughts and imagination and everything, they would instantly go insane and die of shock." I nodded toward Cisco. "Even a mind as gentle as that."

"But isn't that what books do?" she asked. "Good ones?"

I shook my head, then turned to face her. "I think they enable it. Filter it. That's what good books try to do."

She was already eyeing me suspiciously. Catalina tried to look and dress librarian. She wore her glasses on a chain about her neck, but never used them. Her black hair was up, but one heavy lock, as always, found its way free to tumble over her collar. Her lashes were too thick and dark, her lips too full. Even in the nicely cut suit and dangling glasses, there was something a little barmaid about her, like Ava Gardner in *Night of the Iguana*.

"Try?" she replied. "You are so hard on books and their authors, Jack."

"Yes. Try. Trying." I raised my arms. I knew Cisco was listening. "Why else would there be so many? So many new ones coming in? So many old ones being kept around? As long as there are books, I know people are trying to understand one another. That's not so dark."

Cisco took one last deep breath and then went about his re-stacking.

"Speaking of so many books," said Cat. "The burn bin's pretty full. Take it to the incinerator." She sniffed, then wrinkled her nose. "After your shower. Surf good this morning? You smell like a lobster."

I combed my fingers through my hair, the thickness of the salt and sand. "Cat? How many dormant titles have we retrieved? From Tijuana storage?"

"Total?" She pretended to think. "Six. In the three years we've been using Tijuana. Six. Why?"

"I found four floating behind the surf this morning. There might have been more out there."

"Dormants? Are you sure? Ours?"

"I hauled them in and checked their decimals."

She thumbed a note into her cell. At first, I thought she was making a call.

"Have you ever been to the yard," I asked. "Seen the bins?"

Cat shook her head. Another lock of hair fell loose. She tucked it behind her ear. "Have you?"

"No," I answered. "But I'm thinking about it."

"If you go," she said. "I'll come with. Give me those decimals and I'll trace them."

Skilled at dealing with bureaucrats, she was hard to read. She never had trouble looking a person in the eye, speaking in a calm and straightforward manner. Under her leadership, the EPL had prospered. Libraries throughout California liked us, despite the luxurious space of our reading room.

She narrowed her eyes. "Don't worry yet, Jackie Z. I'll take care of it. We can't have books getting in the way of your longboard." She bracketed my shoulders, two firm pats. "Valeria Merced arrives at one. You show her the routine."

"Which routine?"

"The one that doesn't include books in the ocean."

Six

The basement level contained a tiny studio apartment. Catalina, Cisco, and I had all taken turns spending a couple of transitional years living there. It was part of the original architecture, compressed from the start by founders who anticipated the value of space. The conservation room adjoined it. We outsourced most of our repairs, no longer retaining an onsite conservator. But the room still held enough equipment for us to make minor repairs. With nothing more than a bone folder, Cisco could restore spines, press life into the quires.

The vast area of the basement was dedicated to receiving and processing. The loading dock cut into the hillside in the back, one road circling around to the street, another much narrower one heading up the hill to the incinerator. The only vehicle that could squeeze into that path was our little burn shuttle, a golf cart with a hitch for towing the bin.

I showered and changed into my fresh afternoon clothes. After I cinched my tie and tugged my sleeves, I poked around in the closet to see what Catalina was keeping there. A sleeveless green dress hung above a pair of sandals. My suspicions had no direction, only a source—those drowned books.

I heard someone sifting through the burn bin and headed out to the receiving bay. A young woman with short black hair stood peering into the bin. She held a stack of books she had fished out, held them like she was on her way to class. She craned her neck first to see deeper into the bin, then to examine the open mouth of the chute overhead. Though skinny, her arms wrapped the books with strength and expertise. Blue and gray rectangles formed page patterns on her linen dress. She raised one foot for balance as she bent slightly above the bin.

I secured my name badge and approached.

"Those aren't for the taking."

She eased into an upright stance, books cradled. I hit the door switch, and the bay opened, sunlight and salt air surrounding her. She remained still, facing me. I thought of making it a stand-off, of seeing how long she could just hold them.

"Here," I said. I considered her stack. "Let's see what you've tried to spare."

"Spare?"

"I'm about to take them to the incinerator."

She eyed my badge. "What kind of librarian burns books?"

"These aren't really books. Just because it has bound pages with words on it doesn't make it a book."

She raised the stack and with her chin pointed to the top title, Gogol's *Arabesques*.

"We replaced it with a new edition." I motioned upward, then down to the Gogol. "That one's spent."

"I was just going to take them home."

"You don't want to start doing that," I replied. "Certainly not on your first day."

"You know who I am?"

I presented her name badge, given to me by Cat. I used it to jab at the books. She released her books back into the bin where they slid like coins. I watched her pin her badge. Valeria Merced, Librarian, EPL.

"What kind of librarian doesn't know this?" I stirred the air above the bin.

"A different kind of librarian." She eyed the tow cart, the promise of fire. "I want to go with you."

•

VALERIA RODE SHOTGUN AS we drove the burn bath. Jojoba bushes and live oak walled the sides, the cart and trailer fitting neatly. Swallows and purple finches flicked across our view. Behind and below, the ocean hissed and the city thrummed.

"Not a bad death," she said, putting her face to the sun, lashes closed over a long draw of breath.

"This isn't part of the tour."

"Don't give me a tour. I'm a librarian."

I goosed the engine, gaining a rise in the path. "It's not death. This isn't a funeral. We're not building a pyre. It helps me to see a book as a space on the shelf. We're keeping that space alive, letting it sing."

"What about when you read? When you actually read?" She held an imaginary book, hands butterflied. "You still see that space?"

"Sadly, yes."

"After this." She closed her invisible book. "I need to take you on a tour."

"I'm also a librarian," I said.

"Then let's not call it a tour. Let's call it a descent."

"I'm Dante." I navigated a hairpin, tires scuffling. "You're Virgil?"

"Sure." The turn's momentum shoved her shoulder into mine.

"Wasn't he blind?"

"That's Homer. Virgil was the frail one."

"This…descent." I took a quick peek at her neck, then eyed our path. "Did Catalina assign it?"

"You two know each other well."

I could sense her studying my profile. I raised my chin. "What does she want you to show me?"

"The new storage annex for San Diego."

"My schedule's full."

"It isn't an option." She put her hand on my shoulder. It felt like an apology. "You need it. You need to see."

I stopped the cart. The jojoba and live oak compressed, the air thick with their kerosene scent.

"Is this about the books in the ocean? This morning? Did she tell you this morning?"

"Pretty much an ultimatum." She crossed her legs as though she were on a barstool rather than a cart seat. "First day on the job and I get an ultimatum. Thanks to you, Jack."

•

WE REACHED THE PLATEAU that held our incinerator. Cisco named the contraption Cuervo, Spanish for crow. Cisco's imagination was different from mine. Hammered from tin mined from the Baja mountains, the incinerator looked more like a cubist giant, buried waist-deep, arms raised to the sky, mouth open. The two arms formed twin chimneys, the mouth an air intake. It roared when active.

I backed the cart to Cuervo's belly flap. Cisco had taught me how to reverse a trailer, all the counter-intuitive moves and angles, thinking through the pivot. And I taught them to Catalina. Valeria kept looking straight ahead even as we reversed, her eyes locked on the sudden ocean view. Popping out of thick scrub and easing onto ocean overlooks along mountain trails was a Baja phenomenon, one of those opportunities that captured travelers and turned them into natives. Sage gave way to sea air, mountains at your back and shoulders.

After we parked, Valeria strolled to the rim of the plateau. She spread her arms. I knew she would do that. I imagined her doing it the second before she did it. It felt like reading, the way reading used to be for me, before I became this paper Charon.

She tilted her hands as though expecting to fly. If the breeze had been anything more than slight, she might have soared. Her short hair appeared ready for it, her calves flexed for take-off.

"I can see why you stayed." She spoke forcefully because she was still facing away from me. Then she turned to face me, crossed her arms and rubbed her elbows. "Why you didn't advance."

"Advance?"

"Why you didn't go to San Diego. And then let Cat leap-frog you. I read your CV."

I returned to Cuervo and opened his belly flap. I checked inside, making sure no hares or rattlers had found a way in.

"Can I throw the first one in?" she asked. She stepped close, put a hand on my shoulder, joined my search.

"We have to fire it up first." My voice echoed in the tin belly.

"Then can I light the match?" The tin softened her tone, like coming through a radio.

"We're a bit more sophisticated than that. Here," I said, leading her to a side panel.

I showed her how to open the gas line. I let her hit the igniter. Her first punch wasn't hard enough, her pale fist bouncing off the plunger.

"Get mad at it."

She gave it a firm pop, put her shoulder into it. The slight delay had let the gas build up and a soft blue flame spilled from the belly, warmth brushing our faces.

"Any longer and we'd lose our eyebrows," I said as we watched the burner scorch to life, its flames hissing from blue to white. The tin creaked with the sudden heat, up through Cuervo's arms.

She studied my face. "You'd look funny. Without eyebrows."

I escorted her to the edge of the plateau. Her elbow felt cool and smooth, precise. She looked back to the incinerator. "What? Does he just eat them all by himself?"

"We wait. Let it pre-heat. It gets to where they just vaporize if you do it right. Catalina's the master."

"Oh, for a cigarette to make the bus arrive."

I went to the cart and fetched her a Marlboro and a lighter. She squinted at me as she parked the cigarette between her lips. "Cat said you were a health nut. Said you hated getting old."

"These are hers." I replied. "She has stashes all over the library."

I thumbed the lighter and let her bring the cigarette to the flame. She noticed my tremor.

"You look like you could use one of these. I make you nervous?"

I spread my fingers in the smoke of her exhale, let her see the twitch. "Just something I was born with. But yes. I'm wondering if you're going to push me in with the books."

•

Valeria experimented with different ways to burn the titles. An armful at once would momentarily smother the burner. Dark smoke would back up and collect in the flue, then the flames would burst forth, ignite the trapped smoke, and send snowy contrails through the twin chimneys. Handfuls one after another proved the most efficient approach, much the same as stoking a coal-fired engine. A single paperback tossed over the scorching embers flared into oblivion like a magician's trick.

When she came to the Gogol, she hesitated. Wincing, she lifted it toward me.

"It's not a book anymore," I said. "Pages are missing and its spine is fractured. Someone used bacon as a bookmark. Think of it as space. Valuable space."

"It just doesn't feel right this way."

"This way?" I snatched it from her fingers and flipped it into the flames. Within seconds it was white smoke against a blue sky. "You have another?"

We finished the job, alternating chucks. We ignored titles. I stole peeks, mostly of her arms, one of her profile. Her look was wide to the flames, lips parted.

The last book fell to her. A green hardcover, it shifted in her hands, its spine useless, its pages wanting to spill. She opened it.

"Don't do that," I warned.

"Do what?"

"Read one last sentence."

She closed the book, raised her chin. She feigned swiping me with it and followed through by lofting it into Cuervo's belly. For a second, we believed it somehow impervious to the heat as it kept its color and form above the flames, fell into them solid and undaunted. And then it transformed into a sphere of hot white, hissing with a rising wind. We backed away together.

Seven

BACK AT THE LIBRARY, I set Valeria to work in the circle desk. Traffic would be slow until around three. I showed her some of the things that might prove different, mainly how to process her carton while taking care of drop-offs and check-outs.

"Try to be surreptitious when you send them down the chute. Close the flap after."

"Don't want to alarm the patrons," she replied. "Don't let them know what we're really doing." She sniffed the crook of her elbow. "We smell like chimneys."

I sighed. I wanted to be in the ocean. I told her how she had to process her entire carton before she left work, that she'd have to stay late if that's what it took. Most cartons had zero keepers. She had to be decisive. If she set one aside for further consideration, she was taking a risk. Cat's rule was no new carton until the previous one was empty. And no stealing.

"In San Francisco we had staff for assessment," she told me. "They filtered all the litter before titles got to the librarians."

"This is Ensenada," I replied.

"You know, they talk about you up there. Up north."

"Good things, I trust."

"Mostly. Like somewhere you might go to die. In a good way, I mean. Like if you knew you had six months to live. They talk about your reading room. They have photos."

"We work hard," I replied. "Sometimes I surf at lunch, but only for the hour. Cat smokes and works on her sketches in the conservation room. Cisco finds some outside shade and reads. Sometimes we just take walks."

"Together?"

"Not as much as we used to."

•

I FOUND AN EMPTY stacking cart and went about collecting abandoned titles left by morning patrons. I registered each one I found, counting them toward our circulation numbers. This movement felt right after the burning. As I collected the loose titles from the reading room, I pictured Cisco with his cart, somewhere in the upper stacks, re-shelving. His hands were strong from it. Because the decimals were so clear in his head, he reached the spaces quicker than any of us. He could snap a shelf tight and straight with a single tuck and pull. You could hear him in the quiet, the one-two of it, the slip and *thunk*.

My day's carton was haunting me. It was there in the circle with Valeria. I still had fifty-seven titles to assess and the burn demonstration with Valeria had taken time.

I leaned on my cart. It was, as all the reference and wall shelves were, made of wood. From the same source, wood and books went well together. The founders and builders of the EPL understood the value of this. The stacks, however, as in most traditional libraries, were made of metal. This was because stacks were usually part of the infrastructure, holding the building up, linked floor to floor. This was often why libraries struggled with renovation and expansion.

I counted fifteen patrons in the reading room. Most composed on laptops, books stacked or opened around them. Afternoon light split into shafts through the cupola and sifted through the high windows. Valeria manned the desk, Cisco and I pushed our carts, and volumes circulated. Quiet reigned.

•

I FOUND CATALINA IN the conservation room. She had one of the old venting hoods turned on so she could smoke. The fans hummed while she sketched on one of the stand-up desks. Her left hand held a cigarette and braced the top of her pad, while the right brushed charcoal lines on paper.

I placed a damaged book, marked for repair, on one of the mending tables.

"You went and found that," she said without looking up. "So you could come in here and ruin my break. Nothing waits for Jack Zajora when he is troubled."

"You ruined mine. What are you drawing?"

"You."

"Can I see?"

She drew on her cigarette and waved her charcoal over the paper, inviting.

I stood shoulder to shoulder with her and studied her work. It was a book floating in the surf. The water was a pencil gray, the foam circular thumb smudges, the book stark charcoal.

"They weren't like that," I said. "They floated arms-spread, belly-down." I raised my arms wide, one going across her back. "Like this."

She blew a stream of smoke onto her sketch, hard enough to spread like rocket exhaust over the paper. She gave me a hurt and angry look, dark eyes squinting.

"But this looks prettier," I said. "Valeria Merced is not a very good librarian."

"We're not a very good library."

"But she's very good at something."

Cat returned to her brush strokes, bracing the top of the sketch with the angle of her wrist, cigarette perched. "She's a spatial genius. A creature of geometry."

"But a tour, Cat? Sending me back to the minors?"

“Sacramento insists.”

“I thought we were down here because Sacramento would never care. Or see.”

“You and Cisco want to keep your precious reading room, do what they say. Go on that tour and write it up like you just visited Alexandria.”

“Me and Cisco,” I asked. “Not you anymore?”

She drove the charcoal stick hard into the paper, splintering the end and sending shards across the drawing. A heavy tress fell dark over her cheek. “I don’t know what I want anymore, Jack. I don’t know what I can do. What we can do. So just help me keep it going. That’s your genius.”

I stepped back. “You can start your break over. I’ll cover. I like that sketch. It’s better than what I saw. Than what was real.”

She dropped the charcoal and re-did her hair, holding the band with her lips as she raised both hands to gather and spin the black mass. She abandoned the first try, letting it all fall around her face and shoulders, erasing any trace of librarian. She closed her eyes, bowed her head and sighed. Downward, her lashes appeared even thicker. The band almost fell from her lips. I cupped a hand to catch it.

Eight

We called the hour before the 3:00 p.m. rush *the pool.* Cisco must have started it long before Catalina and I came to work at the EPL. Cat imagined it as the water collecting above the cascade. I argued for the game, the quiet felt, the deliberate action of the balls, the hard clicks, the soft drops into pockets. It was a good time to man the circle. You had a desk-mate and the right amount of duty to convince you that you were serving the public well. And there was just enough here and there lull to allow you to attend to your carton.

Valeria's posture was so firm her back didn't touch the chair. She crossed her legs. I pictured those phone operators of old, working the switchboard, speaking into headsets. Drop-offs received a quick hello and thanks, check-outs a brief "enjoy." She said it in Spanish, like a waiter bringing your food—*disfruta.*

Concerned about her assessment rate, I looked for her carton.

"Where's yours?" I asked, dipping into mine.

"Mine's done," she replied. She craned her neck to see my count.

"That's not possible."

She shrugged.

"How many keepers?"

"No keepers."

I stared at her. She looked complete. She gave her short hair a toss, as though clearing bangs.

"I have a system."

"Fast then faster?"

"I'm actually a slow reader. A very slow reader. It takes me a month to read a novel. Whenever I read an especially good paragraph, I stop and spend the day with it. I don't want to read anything else for a while. When I return to the book, I read that paragraph over."

I held the title I had just retrieved from my carton. I thumbed the slick cover while looking at her. Her features, even her earlobes, were pretty and neat. When I didn't respond, she offered me a look of sympathy, the one I was supposed to give her.

"I spent a year reading *Rings of Saturn*. I like to inhabit a book, walk around with it. Dream it."

"Like Gumby and Pokey," I said.

"You're being mean but I can tell you know. You see." She pointed at me, holding her hand eye level, aiming. "Catalina told me what your favorite library is. In the whole wide world."

•

TWENTY-EIGHT YEARS AGO, I met Marisa for the first time in Pátzcuaro's public library. I was traveling Michoacán alone. I needed to escape my training in the L.A. public system, that time when nascent librarians start to believe their job is nothing more than glorified clerk. For escape, Baja was not enough that time. I needed to go deeper into Mexico, to get lost in a mountain state.

Pátzcuaro's library was fashioned from a sixteenth-century church nave. One cavernous room, its arched ceiling was made of timber and the high windows were embedded in thick stucco walls. Small chandeliers ran along the sides, replacing the stations of the cross. The front half of the nave was lined with wooden reading tables, the back half had more reading tables mixed with low oaken shelves. The side walls of the back half held more oaken shelves. Devoted to reading space, the library circulated just a few thousand titles, all hardcovers. The enormous back wall of the nave was covered with a mural depicting Mexico's history, painted by Juan O'Gorman.

Some of the shelf space was devoted to jarred specimens of small animals native to the surrounding volcanic mountains. One jar held the body of a hare found only on the slopes above Lake Pátzcuaro. Curled, eyes closed, the hare slept forever in the quiet of thought and turning pages.

I was staring at that jar when a woman interrupted my emptiness.

"If we removed the lid," said Marisa, "I think it would leap away."

She was tall, American, with short cropped hair dyed blond. She wore a motorcycle jacket and jeans. Her riding boots made her even taller.

"Would you follow?" I asked.

"In a heartbeat."

Readers looked up from their books. The librarian, a man in shirt and tie, shushed us with a finger in front of his smile. With an offering hand, I invited Marisa for a walk outside.

We strolled the calm of siesta, traversing the plaza a few times, then circling its perimeter. Dogs napped. A few city workers smoked on benches, their hands dusted pink from repairing cobblestones.

She was in the middle of a motorcycle trip through Mexico with her boyfriend. She liked Pátzcuaro, he didn't, and so they were to rendezvous in Uruapan.

"Where the river starts there," I told her, "they have these snow-white butterflies the size of napkins. They can hardly fly with those big wings. They kind of plunge then climb, plunge then climb. Makes you dizzy watching."

"We seem to be traveling in opposite directions," she replied.

I told her I was taking this trip to decide if I truly wanted to be a librarian. I was giving myself two weeks. With its odd library and beautiful lake, Pátzcuaro had become my hub. I had already climbed the volcano in Angahuan, visited the monarch sanctuary, ate Tarascan soup in Morelia.

"I wouldn't even go into a library," she told me. "If I were on a walkabout like that."

"I went to see the mural. I like O'Gorman."

She said she preferred Baz Viaud and Siqueiros. She only knew art because she had studied place management at UCLA. Like me, she was in training. "I know about wine and bourbon and flowers," she told me. "I know the psychology of space and light and colors. I studied distance theory."

"I had to study a bit of that," I replied. We stood in the shade of an orange tree. "Librarians, you know? How close to get to the patrons. How to balance professional and friendly. What kind of place do you hope to manage?"

"I plan to do many things," she answered. "Not just one career."

"Makes sense, then." I tapped an orange hanging above us. "To major in spaces. Wherever you are, you're an expert of sorts."

"Librarians should never joke about the occupations of others," she said. She mimed having buck teeth and glasses.

She caught me eyeing her neck, the taper of the buzz cut. The dark roots were more visible there. She palmed her nape and gave me a self-conscious look.

"I cut it for this trip. The wind and all. Derek says he likes it, but I can tell he hates it."

"I know it's not much coming from a librarian." I thought

about performing the buck teeth but refrained. "But I like it. There's a clarity to it."

"Clarity?"

"It's beautiful."

We were twenty-three and lost in Mexico. I was learning to speak the truth about how I felt.

•

VALERIA WORE THE HEADSET so she could answer questions while also entering data for our digital loans. I was still in the circle with her, covering Catalina's break by entering her digitals and running check-outs. Valeria eyed my carton. I had made little progress on it since noon and now we were in the post 3:00 p.m. rush, when double and triple-duty were standard.

"Want me to do yours?" she asked.

"Just answer your call."

"Ensenada Public Library," she said, touching the thin bow of her headset. "How may I help?"

She did not appear to listen to the patron on the other end of the line. She just kept entering data using an odd combination of hunt-and-peck and speed keyboarding. She looked away once to offer a greeting smile to a pair of incoming students. I pictured a hummingbird feeding on a cluster of blossoms.

Then she gave me an exaggerated expression of dismay, indicating the nature of the question she was receiving.

"I'm sorry," she said. "Did you say *human* leather?"

She hummed verification, raised her brow toward me. "One moment, please."

She opened up a new window and went to Google. I made a cutting gesture across my throat. She went to Wikipedia. Again, I slashed at my throat. I rolled my chair next to her, touched her shoulder, and opened up a new window on her screen, one that took her to our own search engine designed by Catalina, one that linked to our reference and periodical holdings. I let her type in "human leather books."

The results scrolled over her screen. She covered her tiny mike with a pinch. "No shit," she said. She uncovered the mike, touched the bow of her headset. "It's known as anthropodermic bibliopegy." She patiently spelled it for her caller. "Yes, up until the late 19th Century, murder victim families were given court records bound in the tanned skin of the executed culprit. Yep, a daughter's murder would be bound in the skin of her killer."

She listened, watching me, then crimping the skin on the back of my hand. She wrinkled her nose.

"No, ma'am," she said. "We don't have any here."

She ended the call.

"Don't hang up on them," I told her.

"Why do they have to call?" She opened her hands. "Why do we answer?"

"Some people still need to hear a voice," I replied. "To talk. You should have told her where to find one."

"I don't want to know."

"Look," I told her. "I don't know how it is in San Francisco these days, but we have to keep doing some things—things that libraries have always done—in order to make us still matter. Otherwise, we're just doing things like this." I pointed to my carton and her list of digital loans. "Things that make us irrelevant."

"I would rather be the agent of my own obsolescence," she replied. "Than have some other power do it for me."

Nine

DURING A LULL, SHE kicked at my carton. The patterns of light on the wood floor of the foyer told me it was just after four. The wood was red fir, a bit soft for flooring but it helped with the quiet. The builders of the EPL believed it would be the right combination of clean and reflective, that it would enhance the glow of the Baja day, render it thoughtful, meditative even.

"Why don't you go have a cigarette?" I suggested.

"I don't really smoke," Valeria answered.

"Neither does Cat. Go help yourself to one of her stashes. That one I showed you in the tow cart."

"What if she catches me?" Valeria pointed to the basement beneath us. "Down there."

"Tell her how insufferable I am. She'll most likely join you."

•

I WAITED FOR HER to leave before I dipped into my carton. I resisted the urge to leave the circle and venture into the reading room, to wander there. I waited for her to take the time to light the cigarette, pictured her smoking near the open bay door, her back to the burn bin. Then I chose three books from my carton that appeared to be fast rejects. Slick covers, perfect binding, unyielding gutters, generic fonts, thoughtless sentences, indulgent titles. I spent a minute on the first, less on the second, a little more on the third. I slid them down the burn chute, one minute apart.

When I opened the flap the third time, I discovered that she had sent an exhale of smoke up the chute. I was fifty-one.

I had a fifteen-year marriage and a ten-year divorce on my life CV. I was hoping to go surfing at Brigadoons after work, sip tequila and look for gray whales at sunset. And I was playing Chutes & Ladders with a kid who seemed to hold my fate in her quick fingers.

I checked out a stack of books for a high school student, a boy with big glasses and an Adam's apple as prominent as his nose. He wore a sweater vest over his T-shirt and seemed proud of his eclectic stack—three titles on card-counting, one about the history of dragons, and two on chess strategies.

"You can borrow one more," I told him. "Our limit's seven."

He adjusted his glasses.

"Here." I fished a title from a stack I had re-entered. *Sirens: A Photographic History of Influential Icelandic Women.* "Add this."

He nodded and took what I gave him.

I peered into my carton. I still had more than thirty titles to go. I chose a volume that would take some work, some reading. It was a hardcover novel with a jacket by a designer whose work I recognized. The publisher was big and had put some money behind it, at least in the beginning. But it was already a year old, which was odd, indicative of the abandoned. It was *Equisa*, by J.B. D'Acquisto, an author I had never heard of.

The jacket cover featured a picture of a corner torn from a page. The only print on the torn paper formed the last three letters of some word that ended in *u r e.* The font made these letters appear typed on an old Smith-Corona. The fragment of paper rested in the palm of a woman's hand. The torn edge of the paper was translucent. It was easy to imagine a breeze blowing, ready to carry the fragment away.

I read the first paragraph:

> Prima X—Equisa—honors her cousin's request and scatters his ashes over the caldera of Paricutín. The wind is perfect, swirling lightly around the volcano's lip, taking him in a procession of dust devils down the inside slope and over the green lake at the bottom. Steam filters up through the pumice, forming wisps that go into the blue sky and disappear. She marvels at this, one parade down, one up, and then at the geometry of the gray cinder cone resting atop its apron of black lava. She feels herself a point along the sharp edge of the cone, invisible unless you measure her against something. The sky, the green lake, the stark line where the lava meets the pine woods.

I rested my eyes on the library entrance, on the late afternoon light and the bougainvillea beyond. I was about to sample another paragraph somewhere in the middle of the text when I realized Valeria had returned to the circle. It was as though she had risen through the chute and was just there.

"My word," she said. "You're reading."

I closed the novel. I weighed it with both hands.

"Do we have a keeper?" she asked, returning to her chair.

I dropped *Equisa* into the chute. I pictured her as a dark point near the broken tip of a gray triangle. I imagined her keeled back against her sharp descent, maintaining a perfect vertical to the base. Lava pushed over a forest.

Valeria gave me a suspicious look, then eyed the lid of the chute.

"I know you think I just dumped my carton down the chute. To impress you and Cat." She put on her headset and took her seat, straightening her back and shoulders. "That I just saw the whole mass as fuel for Cuervo. But I considered every single title. I mean, I admit that I want to go on the very next burn run. I kind of can't wait, in fact. But I was responsible in my assessment."

"Right," I said. "Your system."

Again, she looked at the chute lid, then to me, as though she thought I was about to dive into it.

"Yes," she replied. "And at least I remove all emotion from the equation. Unlike some."

A checkout line had formed in front of my station. She had an incoming call flashing. More readers were entering, some hauling returns. I thought of a procession of dust devils composed of human ash.

Ten

My hours were nine to six, with an hour for lunch. Like most public employees, I pulled extra duty, a little before, a lot after. Cisco always remained until our 9:00 p.m. closing, taking care of the day's odds and ends. And I never really knew when Catalina left, though often, from a night perch along the burn path, I would see her silhouetted against the yellow square of the bay door, having a last smoke, the rest of the building gone dark hours earlier. So, it was not unusual for me to still be at work with the clock nearing 6:30.

But this time I felt very self-conscious because I was taking care of my assessment carton while Cat and Valeria worked the circle desk. We all tried our hardest to avoid this particular ignominy. Mine was the only carton left. Ordinarily I would have dragged the box down to the basement and finished the shameful ritual in isolation, but I also had Catalina's data entry to complete. And I wanted company, judgmental or not.

I was thinking of Cousin X. Prima Equisa. Equisa. That paragraph abandoned her on the slope of that cinder cone. Where would the next paragraph take her? I could sense from the images in the first that she would move fast and far. I imagined her an outlaw of sorts.

I released three rejects into the burn chute, waiting for each one to finish its drop before releasing the next, giving them a bit of final respect. Cat and Valeria had their backs to me, pillars of responsibility.

Catalina spoke into her work, keyboard still clicking. "Take it downstairs, Jackie Z. We get it."

"He's afraid of being alone." Valeria was still wearing the headset. It looked like she was answering a caller.

I had ten titles to go. I sloshed them around, picturing them coalescing into one at the dark bottom of the carton. I told Cat and Valeria that I never understood the fear of being alone.

"He just doesn't remember," said Cat.

When I had finished both tasks, I said *buenas noches, mis madrinas* and hauled my empty box down to recycling. I dowsed all the basement lights save for the pallid bulb above the burn bin. I gave the rejected volumes a stir, thinking that if *Equisa* appeared from the swirl I might steal away with it. It did not. I dug further with the next stir, elbow-deep. I spied the telltale jacket design, the palm holding the feathery page fragment: *u r e.*

As though playing jackstraws, I slid the book free of the others. The overhead bulb swayed in a draft. The rejects whispered over one another. A rectangle of light flashed atop the pile and I peered up the chute, listened for the flap.

I left *Equisa* on the surface, visible to someone looking down the chute. From a window above the bay door, the sulfurous light of low sun crossed the loading area in a single shaft. A patron's footsteps sounded above as I ambled into the basement's dimness. I matched my own steps to the rhythm and direction. Everything in that first paragraph pulled vertical, at once rising and dropping. The dust devils, composed of death but come alive, descended toward the lake while their ashy forms rose. The cinder cone pointed skyward as Equisa's form drove downward on its slope. The dark lava bed loomed beneath airy blue sky.

How could any reader escape such a trap, his imagination stretched to the snapping point? How could any reader abandon such a devoted protagonist? And a cousin, nonetheless. The Ensenada *prima* we all have, who waits with the money that is owed, who can fix your engine for a better price, who is that woman you were with.

I returned to the bin and swiftly stole *Equisa* from atop the pile. I cinched the book beneath my belt, where it pressed cool against my lower back. I draped my untucked shirt about my waist. There are no rats in the library. Cisco has always seen to that. Once in a while a bull snake slinks its way into the basement, drawn by the curious scent of paste and binding. So maybe that was what I heard, a slither in a dark corner.

In Spanish, I whispered their names into the dimness: Cisco? Catalina? Valeria?

The only answer came from the overhead footsteps, from readers leaving with their borrows.

I considered tossing *Equisa* back into the bin, of making a show of it by flipping it high so it would open before it tumbled and rattled like a wounded pigeon. But I left the EPL through the basement exit, a stolen pressing the base of my spine.

Eleven

I MADE IT TO Brigadoons too late for any surfing, too late to even climb down the path. The sun had just set, yellowing the sky with that false light that fools us into thinking we can see. The horizon still burned in a white line above the ocean. The last surfers, their dark forms hunched and waiting, speckled the swells. The waves crashed unseen, but their salt spray carried heavy on the updraft. It was all I could do to resist clambering down the cliff-side, stripping on the wedge of beach, running headlong into the breakers.

I still carried the stolen *Equisa* with me, afraid to leave it in my car, the way you might fear abandoning an instrument in the back seat. I held the book with the cover pressed to my hip. Some surfers were already returning from the sea. Their boards thudded against rock as they climbed. Their voices, hushed over by the shore break, rose wordless but filled with inflection, tones of devotion and wonder.

When the first group made it to the final landing, I stopped them from tossing their boards up the final eight-foot rise. I could hear them but not see them. Night pooled early in the pockets of the black cliffs.

"Is that you, Jackie Z?" one of them asked.

I called them quitters and then had them pass their boards up to me, where I could ease them over the rocks and lay them gently in the roadside sand. The last board from the group, rising from the shadows, I recognized as Flaco's.

After I had aligned their boards in the sand, the Brigadoons rose from the darkness of the ledge. Still in their wetsuits, they appeared hewn from the black rocks, shadows released. Flaco looked down at the neatly arranged boards, all four going left to right according to length.

"Always the librarian," he told the others.

I could tell they were pros because they were looking back to the sea, tracing the swells, gauging the horizon's clarity, searching for some promise for tomorrow. Flaco noticed the book in my hand, again the front cover hidden against my hip. He tapped the spine.

"That one of those?" he asked. "From this morning? Looks in good shape."

"Did you see any more?" I pressed the book closer to my hip.

He shook his head. He put his arm around my shoulders and rocked me toward him. We eyed the horizon together. The other Brigadoons peeled off their wetsuits, broke them down around their waists. I envied what they must have felt, the coolness and lightening. Flaco let go of me and shucked the top half of his wetsuit. He smelled of salt and kelp.

Three more surfers rose from the ledge. They appeared short next to Flaco. They were young and kind of danced on the balls of their feet, proud to have conquered the day's swell.

"Where are your boards?" I looked at them, then to Flaco.

"Oh, we're coming back," the stockiest one told us. "First thing tomorrow. We stashed our sticks in the cliff." He tapped his temple to show us how clever they were, how they were always thinking.

I checked Flaco, to see if he wanted me to tell them. The other Brigadoons waved bye and headed up the roadside toward their van. Evening had gathered. Most of the light seemed to be coming from the sea rather than the sky. Flaco's features were hollows and shadows. I couldn't really discern his expression. I went by the tilt of his head.

"Smart," I said to the rookies. I opened my arms to Flaco. "Why didn't we think of that?"

Flaco shrugged.

The rookies left, clapping each other on their backs. In the morning, their boards would be gone, taken by the tide. Even if they had stashed them high, they would be gone. The night tide would rise about a third of the way up the cliffs, the winter swell sending rockets of seawater into the sky, blasting the rocks clean, the mist dampening the highway. It was a thing to come and watch and listen to these ocean geysers, a Baja event. They played like a calliope when the tide crashed at its highest and roughest, the many different cliff funnels varying the notes and volume.

Flaco, now alone with me, motioned to the book. "Funny. I never see you with one of those."

"I try not to take my work home with me."

"So what makes this one so special?" With two fingers, he pried the book away from my hip. "This. This Equisa."

"Nothing. I brought it here to throw it into the sea."

"Equisa," he said. "An X-Woman?"

"*Prima Equisa*," I replied. "Actually. Just another cousin. Cousin X."

I readied myself into a discus throwing stance, the book in the crook of my wrist. Flaco stilled me.

"I'll take it."

"You don't read novels."

A board came flying over the ledge and landed at our feet. We watched a lone figure climb from the rocks. It was a young woman, her wetsuit glistening black, hair slicked back. She was panting from her last ride and swift ascent. Hands on knees, she gulped air.

"Did you have a good last ride?" Flaco asked her.

She looked at us, the ocean twilight reflecting on her face. She grinned, big and toothy, almost a laugh but for her gasping. It made us want to return to the waves. It made us want to be young enough to start all over.

Twelve

Seven cliff-side terraces, linked by staircases cut into the stone, formed Calafia. The main kitchen and bar stood at the top. As splendid as it appeared, especially at night, the architecture and structuring were simple, determined by the cliff and the sea. The waitresses made Calafia work, ferrying trays up and down the escarpment, delivering Jimbo's elegant margaritas with a mountain climber's endurance, a dancer's lilt. Marisa and Jimbo understood this and paid their staff well. They were the last in a long line of Calafia owners, but they were the only ones who made the place a success.

At night, you could watch from afar, positioned on a bend in the Baja highway. The fiery kitchen at the top, the waitresses descending the dark escarpment with candled trays, a curving strand of flickering light connecting the torch-lit plateaus. Laughter rose above the low thunder of the surf.

I chose a table three landings up from the sea, where the ocean mist drifted softly above the torches. Where I could be alone, just before the dinner crowds came trickling down. By candlelight and the sound of waves, I re-read the opening paragraph of *Equisa* and then ventured further:

> Prima X—Equisa—honors her cousin's request and scatters his ashes over the caldera of Paricutín. The wind is perfect, swirling lightly around the volcano's lip, taking him in a procession of dust devils down the inside slope and over the green lake at the bottom. Steam filters up through the pumice, forming wisps that go into the blue sky and disappear. She marvels at this, one parade down,

one up, and then at the geometry of the gray cinder cone resting atop its apron of black lava. She feels herself a point along the sharp edge of the cone, invisible unless you measure her against something. The sky, the green lake, the stark line where the lava meets the pine woods.

She makes the hike back across the lava beds in under three hours, but stops in Angahuan only to have a tortilla, canned sardines, and a cactus pear soda before catching a bus north. She is already tallying the inheritance her cousin left her, all his savings from his work in the Tijuana quarry. She rides the green vinyl seats bus instead of the black one with curtains and AC.

When the bus reloads after a stop somewhere in the desert, Equisa finds herself sitting next to something new. She looks back among the passengers to find her former seatmate. The woman, discovered, looks away. Equisa can tell from the swift turn of chin how much money the woman accepted to switch seats. For the first time Equisa sees the other side of the woman's profile and notes that there is a mole where the end of her eyebrow should be. It forms a supine exclamation mark at the base of her furrowed brow. Equisa watches it flex; with thoughts of newfound money it flexes and exclaims.

Her new seatmate wears a white *campesino* hat and a new work shirt blue enough to remind her of the sky above Paricutín. Sitting a notch too close, he wears cologne which she at first mistakes for bus ozone.

He smiles at her. His teeth all slant one way as though once struck by a mighty blow. He has a dark brown splotch on that side of his jaw. The rest of his skin is creamy. All the Mexican is in that one splotch. She isn't surprised to hear an accent, German, or that his breath smells of mint over bus stop beer. I believe I have something that you need. He uses the subjunctive.

She looks down at the space between his hip and hers, waiting for the appearance. His pale hand moves in, palming a torn corner of paper filled with words. He curls his fingers before she can read.

How much?

How much pages? Or how much monies? He winks, but with both eyes at the same time. She has seen this before, from people who can't do it with just one.

Pages.

Three hundred nine. His slanted teeth grind the sounds. *Tres. Cien Nueve.*

And money?

This corner is free for you. And the rest is free too for you when you find it. Just across the border in a house in San Ysidro. The yellow house on Vidrio Street. The whole thing waits for you. He presses the corner of paper into her open hand.

I read more, lost count of the pages turned.

She lived in a world where paper was more valuable than gold, where a torn piece of corner was worth the cost of a smuggled emerald. I rested my eyes on the black sea.

From behind, footsteps descended. And then Marisa's arms wrapped my chest and shoulders, her perfume a trace within the salt air. Her breasts softly pinched my neck.

"Hey," I whispered. "What are you doing?"

When I tilted back my head to see her, she kissed me on the lips, her tongue to mine. At first, I surrendered. She held the kiss long enough to steal my breath and then I got nervous, lips tensing.

She laughed, our chins bumping.

"No one's down here. Just us."

"The waitresses," I said. "They're light on their feet."

"They pretty much know." Marisa tried for another kiss.

I twisted away.

"Don't worry," she said. "I'm the one who gives them their checks and vacations."

A night gull cawed. I pretended to look for it, peering into the darkness beyond the torch.

She said fine and stood as though ready to take my order. With the back of her knuckles, she tapped my stolen book.

"That's an odd title."

"It's an odd book."

She bent down for a closer look, flipped the cover. Our necks were close, her perfume something like tobacco leaf.

"Wait a second. You took this. This isn't a library holding. You snitched this."

I closed the book and pushed it away from her. I eased my head to her shoulder.

"What are you up to, Jack?" She held still for me, crouched. "What's going on? You don't answer my texts all day but show up here anyway. You sit here like you can see the grays out there in the darkness. Like you're listening for them. You read a stolen. By candlelight."

She slid her hand to the center of my chest. I held it.

"A quiet night?"

"No doubt," she said. "Word gets out when Jimbo's in L.A."

"Can I come back and pick you up later?" I kissed her forearm. "Let me know when?"

•

WE DID NOT HAVE an affair in Pátzcuaro while Derek waited in Uruapan. That afternoon, after we strolled the plaza outside the Pátzcuaro library, we did ride to the ruins of Tzintzuntzan on her motorcycle. In order to get us clear of the city, she drove first. She let me drive the clear roads to the pyramids. We switched places in a turnout to a cemetery. The graves were still decorated with marigolds from *Los Días de Los Muertos*. The heaps of flowers had started to wilt and their pasty scent hung heavy in the air.

"I want to look you up when I return to L.A.," I told her. "I'm saying this now because I don't want to talk about anything when we get to the ruins."

"Anything?" She was eyeing the cemetery, how it banked up the hillside and how the dead flowers trapped the afternoon sun.

"Anything other than what we see around us."

I drove her bike to Tzintzuntzan. She wrapped her arms about my ribs and pressed her face to my nape as we ducked into the wind. Legend claimed that Tzintzuntzan meant "place of the hummingbirds" in the language of the Tarascans, the three syllables evoking the zig-zag buzz of flight. The pyramids and sacrificial platform stood hushed and empty amid fields thick with wildflowers. There were more dragonflies than hummingbirds. The hum of wings intensified the quiet. In moments, we held hands. At times we would separate to explore alone, kick some stones. Later that year, when we got together in Los Angeles, she asked me why I didn't kiss her there, in the place of the hummingbirds.

Thirteen

I WENT TO ONE of the infinite number of points along the Baja peninsula where, at night, you could sense you were standing at the edge of the world, a world sailing through space. Below and beyond was all darkness. The sea wind and the surf made the cutting sound of a wake. The running light of a distant fishing boat floated in the black.

Had I taken that San Diego job ten years ago, I would have no immediate access to these overlooks. And Marisa needed them at least as much as I did, though she might never admit this. I learned so much about myself through her. She revealed my own need and use for spaces—Brigadoons, the EPL reading room, this cliff top.

The dreams of my lifetime were not yet faded. But they had been refracted. I was a decent California librarian, but the Baja version. I loved Marisa and I believed she still loved me, but she was with another. I took care of books, but that involved destroying them or, at least, not saving them. I still read, but there was always some calculation to it. Cisco claimed we were defined by our hopes. To see my hopes, to see myself, was to see a stick half in water.

The surf lulled and the wind quit. Whenever these particular caesuras happened, the Brigadoons would sit on their boards and offer theories. The Earth wobbled on its axis, the tide shifted, the moon achieved opposition, a butterfly crossed the equator, the gods got lazy. From above and in the dark, the sensation intensified, pulled through me, a sudden and thus palpable deafness.

I recalled the sound of a page being turned, imagined it

out there in the darkness, a furtive and beckoning snap. There was a warmth in the crackle. Could I live in Equisa's world? A world without that sound?

•

IN THE BASEMENT STUDIO of the library, I lay with Marisa. A desk lamp in the far corner, neck bent toward the floor, cast the only light. Otherwise, the entire library, above and here below, was dark. In that glow, no more than a monk's reading candle, we sought one another in a kind of Brownian motion, given over to the faintest of outside forces.

Her arm rested diagonally across my torso, her thumb shaping to my pelvis.

"I never feel we're alone here," she said.

"You know why so many libraries are said to be haunted?"

"Don't scare us, Jack." She blew a cool breath over my chest. "This is nice."

"But that's just it," I said. "They're not haunted. It's the books. The ones that are never moved or even touched. They swell and contract. They decompose. They morph. All very slowly, imperceptibly, but eventually they will push one another over. Or make a carousel twirl a bit. Or just sigh."

"Oh, yes," she replied. "Thanks. That's much more reassuring."

Undefined in the dimness, the ceiling pressed down on us. For a long while, we heard nothing—not the ocean, not the city, no nearby traffic, no ghosts or sad books. The Ensenada Public Library was quiet. Finally, from far off, a dog barked twice, followed by the chuckling of a ground owl somewhere up the hillside.

"That book," she murmured. "*Exina*. The one you're squirreling around."

"*Equisa*," I corrected. "It's nothing."

"What's it about?" she asked. "This nothing."

"Equisa is some kind of archivist. She lives in a world without paper and ink. Books are impressions of books. They come in a kit. You drink a tea and flip through these placards. And that's how we read."

"We?"

"People in her world. She acquires what seems like the last remaining scrap of paper and ink. It's just a torn corner with the letters *u-r-e* on it, the end of some word. She's trying to smuggle it somewhere."

"Where?" Marisa raised her head from my shoulder.

"Up from Michoacán to San Ysidro."

"The border?"

"Yeah, but I'm not sure there are borders anymore. I mean, the borders might all be cyber borders or something. Like Mexico is now just as important as America—the US, I mean. Currency—the stuff she uses to get things, papery things or just clothes—is just passed around with cell phones."

"Clothes?" Marisa shifted onto her stomach, propped chin to hands.

"She loses all her clothes in the middle of the desert. People—like these sort of pseudo DEA people—attack her and maybe take that scrap she acquired."

"Why don't you just accept the book and enter it into the system?"

"I'm making it sound better than it is. It's kind of a mess. She uses all these bits of theories to save herself, or at least reassure herself. She uses Oulipo word games. Things like that."

"Reassure?" asked Marisa. "Maybe that's the word. The torn-off word."

"Yeah," I said. "The story tricks you into making guesses like that."

She rolled onto her back, getting some distance. Where she had been pressed to me suddenly felt cold and empty.

"You're not even supposed to judge it like that. Just enter it, Jack. Then check it out and read it. Like everybody else."

I started to explain but she put her hand over my lips.

"That's it, isn't it? Everybody else." She smothered my mouth with her palm. "This way you can keep it to yourself. Your so-important librarian self."

She released her hand from my lips, but I had nothing to say.

"Remember how you used to read to me?" she asked. "Like this?" She opened her arms above us.

"Only when we traveled," I replied.

"This is traveling, Jack. Read to me."

Fourteen

I READ TO HER the part I had failed to explain. I kept waiting for her to stop me, but she lay still and listened. Whenever I stole a glance, I could see Marisa's pensive expression, her lips sometimes moving as though she were the one reading.

I began where the coyote passes the scrap to Equisa during her bus ride north.

> This corner is free for you. And the rest is free too for you when you find it. Just across the border in a house in San Ysidro. The yellow house on Vidrio Street. The whole thing waits for you. He presses the corner of paper into her open hand. They'll ask you to describe me. I think you can describe me.
>
> She has been reading the same antique cereal box fragment for the past week. She knows all about the plight of giant pandas just before their extinction. On her journey with the ashes, she tried to trade the scrap several times for anything new. In Morelia she tried at a café she'd heard about, and in Zamora she tried once in the old bowling alley that is now a museum full of jars, and once in a pizza joint she'd heard about. At the pizza place she almost fell for a con, an old one, where the words were just words and the paper wasn't authentic paper.
>
> Her new seatmate leans back, folds his arms across his chest, and covers his eyes with his hat. She craves reading the corner scrap he passed her. But she knows the rules and waits for the next stop, hopes he will leave then, or at least change seats. She eyes the passengers, looks for

another like herself. How might they look? How does she look? Everyone else is staring into their laps, a shine in their eyes, an occasional fingertip to the ear. At times, they turn to the window and glance at the desert. At times, they look at her.

And there is no one else like her on this green vinyl seats bus going all the way to Tijuana. No one else who can read from paper. No one else who can read for more than twenty seconds at a time. She wants to ask the sleeping coyote next to her if he can read from paper, if he can read what he just gave her, if he can read the three hundred nine pages from which it was torn. She catches a waft of his cologne, his breath of mint and Modelo, and knows the answer.

The sleeping coyote slants further into the seat and his hat skids down with each breath, until it rests in the crook of his folded arms, rising and falling on his chest. Equisa craves the words on paper tucked into her jeans, carefully into the coin pocket, spread to the cloth, shaped to the cloth, the feel of the cloth. She has not even registered the language, only the curves, lines, and angles of the black letters, the soft white bed of the parchment. She brims with the promise of the corner full of new words, of the whole it will connect her with.

The coyote sleeps deeply, dreaming something fast and thrilling, his lashes lifting sometimes to reveal his whites rolled back and searching. He's somewhere else she thinks. Now she is unclear on the rules—which she knows as well as anyone—or is convincing herself of their vagueness. She knows you wait until he is gone. Until his body is gone. It's for his safety and for the safety of what he has just sold her.

But the craving and the promise inside her are very strong. She knows the scrap is legitimate because his payment awaits him, delivered after she arrives, performs. She reads the panda cereal box again. She tries different things, fitting in anagrams, applying n+7 and other tricks of the Oulipou. The panda eats a particular bamboo found only in the Chinese forest. The pandit teas a particular bandarilla found only in the Sinchee foretoken.

She smiles at how this makes sense, how it is more interesting. You could tea a bandarilla, sink it into something. And a pandit might very well be someone who would do that. And he would also be one who could find something in a foretoken. And she smiles more at how the sentence is about her on this green bus somewhere in the middle of the Durango desert. What she has in her coin pocket is a foretoken. The pandit snoozes beside her, plunging bandarillas in his dreams, dreams fed by the foretoken he has passed to her.

The Oulipou were right, way back then. It's all in the words, all about the words, and the paper that receives them. Every reader should've listened. The Oulipou should've been more convincing, not so playful.

An especially active moment of the coyote's dream causes his arms to flop and release the hat. The hat tumbles across his belly and into her lap, upside down. She sees that other passengers have noticed this, the fate of his hat. What will she do?

She waits the twenty seconds it takes before their eyes turn away. But other eyes find her and the hat, those eyes following the gaze of others, a long series of twenty second waits. An endless loop perhaps. The woman with the exclamation mark eyebrow finds her. Equisa counts to twenty and then does something simple and brilliant, something that takes care of everything for the moment.

She continues cradling the hat politely, propping it with the fingers of her outside hand. Secretly with her inside hand, she removes the scrap from her coin pocket, palms it, and lets it drop unnoticed into the hat as she raises her hand to sweep her hair behind her ear. The fumy cologne rises from the brim of the hat. The corner scrap steeps in it.

But she can smell the paper, the ink. She closes her eyes, inhales, sifts through the grime from the bus's rubber floor, the oil of the gear box, the hot metal of the gear box, the cakey pollen of marigolds from a passenger two seats up by a cracked window, the Modelo and mint sleep-breaths of the coyote, the immediate rise of sweat and cologne from the hat brim. And she finds them, the ink first. The ink smell is the air of a dream, damp and tannic. She swims in it, imagines the cool cloud released by an octopus. They once wrote with that ink. It worked well, and all that squid and octopus in the Mediterranean. The only problem was that it drew bugs and worms. It tasted too good.

Then rises the paper, fibrous through the ink, the remaining moisture of the ink wetting it, making that wet paper smell, clay, clay thoughts. Ink retains at least some of its moisture for the duration of its existence. When it loses the last molecules of moisture, it's no longer ink and falls off the page, dust on your shelves. Really good ink seals itself and lasts who knows how long. Then they started using lasers and that just scorches the paper. No ink.

Equisa peeks only at the very top word on the wedge of words before she reaches into the hat and palms the scrap, returns it to her coin pocket. She decides this quick taste and smell, this brief infusion, is fair. The coyote is away in a dream, with her in body only. So she feels it's fair to resist the body of the scrap while experiencing a bit of the dreaming it offers. Still cradling his hat, she closes her eyes and reads the top word, which is merely a fragment of a word, its front end torn: *u r* e.

Three of her favorite letters—either in Spanish or English. The shapes of the first and second contrast into the golden ratio. The second forms a perfect upside-down incompletion of the first. Then the third introduces the promise of a circle, cuts it off and tries to go back, and within the resulting shape implies the golden ratio again. The first mirrors its capital, a proud child. The next two reinvent themselves, hardly even shadows of their capitals, maybe at least crumpled high noon shadows of their capitals. She lets herself indulge in these metaphors; they are exact enough and they efficiently describe the indescribable shape and impact of these letters, letters that have no remaining referents other than sound, other than the shapes they force upon our lips, teeth, and tongues: *u r* e.

Recalling the scent of ink and paper, the salty warm swim with the octopus, she considers some of the many possibilities. Allure rapture capture sure—a name even. Saussure, someone she studied at UNAM. She doesn't even realize if her eyes are opened or closed. She is following the contours and scents of the letters, sliding herself over their crests and down their chutes.

But in the bottom corner of Chihuahua the bus must navigate things go wrong. Her eyes are definitely open and the sun is close to setting behind a distant bluish sandstorm. The bus stops at a sun-bleached station with corrugated steel over its windows and a shattered solar panel on its roof. But there is a new-looking baño sign on one edge of the building and so when the driver cranks open the door, passengers start to get out. Equisa and the coyote are fifth and sixth in line exiting the bus. She sees that there are more one-story buildings, tracts and tracts of them spanning all the way to the blue sandstorm. It's one of those places that just gets big, never gets a set name, never becomes a city, but just gets big. It's one of those places and this station is on the edge.

As soon as the coyote steps off the bus behind her, the driver cranks the door closed and rumbles away, leaving the six passengers arms-spread and spinning in a kind of sandstorm of their own. Then four people appear from the side of the building where the baño sign is. One, a skinny young man, carries what looks to be a torn half of a bicycle. He circles behind the coyote and impales him with the bike-thing and jumps back. The coyote falls backward, straight, and the ground shoves the bike half deeper. The wheel presses all the way to his spine and he is balanced like that, arms spread, punctured chest to the sky. The coyote's eyes are opened and his one-way slanted teeth are gnashed. Two of his breaths pass up through the end of one of the bike frame tubes, two blow-notes in a bottle.

The four ambushers let the other passengers run away, but the skinny youth and another catch Equisa before she can even move. They hold her arms, each one grasping with both hands, and turn her toward the leader who is a woman in a uniform windbreaker—maybe stolen, maybe issued, maybe stolen then issued, maybe she doesn't know. Another man stands there. The windbreaker woman nods to that man and he searches Equisa for the scrap.

Another blow-note sounds from the coyote. His eyes are open, unblinking, beginning to skin over with dryness in the desert air. She looks to the sandstorm in order to endure the search. Endure.

The sandstorm is boiling sideways along the horizon of single-story buildings. It's the color of the corrugated steel that covers the windows. The sun's image wavers behind it, melts through in bursts. Her body is jostled, swatted, prodded with the man's heavy fingers. He begins to knead into her clothes, the folds and pockets.

No time for that, the woman says. Strip her and take her clothes.

He finds the cereal box scrap with the panda text when he yanks down her jeans. The panda eats a particular bamboo found only in the Chinese forest. The pandit teas a particular bandarilla found only in the Sinchee foretoken. She looks at the impaled coyote, balanced on the wheel, arms spread in final wonder. One more *ooooo*-sound bubbles from one of the metal tubes piercing his chest. It is mournful, and for her.

The man flings her clothes back toward the windbreaker woman. The two boys continue their holds on Equisa's arms and now they are looking at her naked body, back, front, back, front. Then they get out of sync and it's one back, the other front. One front, the other back, tick-tocking that way as the woman eyes the cereal box scrap.

This isn't it. This is nothing. This isn't even paper. He

wouldn't sell her this. She wouldn't bargain for this. She burns it with her lighter and the paint from the cardboard, the paint of the black and white words and the black and white panda face burns in multicolored flames, green, blue, and deep orange.

The man's fingers are inside her. It feels worse to feel the boys looking at her in that tick-tocking way.

That's enough, windbreaker woman tells him. It can't be any place moist. Don't be an idiot. Her hair. Search her hair.

Equisa feels his fingers go into her hair, feels them rake her skull. He tries to comb his fingers through but she hasn't washed or brushed it since before her volcano climb. Some ashes are in there, in those snarls and cool black pockets. He tries again.

No time for that either, says the woman. Cut it off and bundle it with the clothes. He uses a big knife to saw off her hair in one massive clump. One of the boys holding her rubs himself against her thigh as he watches this shearing.

No time for that, says the woman. You stab him if he does that again. You stab him.

Equisa is relieved the blade is sharp and her hair goes easily. Her head lightens. She lets her head lighten. She watches the distant sandstorm turning purple as the sun lowers behind it. Fragments of wind thrown from the storm hurry through this raid. She feels the breeze on her skin and on her scalp, on her scalp for the first time she can ever remember.

The man tosses the bundle of hair to the woman. She catches it and cradles it with the clothes. I'm certain it's in here somewhere. Somewhere in all this. As she turns to stride away she says to the boys, strangle her and bury her in the sand.

Can we take our time?

If you do, you have to walk back. We leave now. She strides to some place behind the building and the man hurries after her, sheathing his knife.

One of the boys throws his belt over Equisa's head and cinches it around her throat. He leads her to a sandy patch just off the road where the other boy is scraping out a grave with his forearms. Equisa makes an effort to look after the coyote, to give him that bit of respect. His slanted teeth gnash at the sky, his arms question the wide universe, and his eyes petrify.

The boy with the belt yanks her into the scoop and she goes into the sand knees first. The other boy undoes his pants. Equisa closes her eyes. She hears the other boy unzip and a truck starting up and peeling away, its tires making a throaty choking sound over the crumble of the road shoulder.

The boy yanks the belt and says open your eyes, open your eyes. You have beautiful eyes and we want to see them. She doesn't open them and feels the belt collapse around her throat. She inhales softly through her nose, finding passageways that seem new in there, around and behind her vocal chords.

u r e. *Endure* is no longer enough. *Endure* won't work. It would end in death, closure.

The belt pulls her into the grave. The sand shapes itself along her spine, her curves. She feels the other boy's mouth on her toes. His tongue is cold and limp, a fake one, she thinks, a prosthetic. What is the word? There is one. What is the word? she asks them, out loud. The belt goes slack for moment, the mouth leaves her toes. There is one, I know.

Open your eyes! The belt tightens, pulling her head

into the sand, but she has stolen a healthy breath.

With the dose of air feeling its way through her body, a cool cloud of ink in warm salt water, her thoughts sharpen. When she finds the word she opens her eyes. It remains silent behind her eyes. Conjure.

Conjure.

Out loud, to the sky, she says: The panda eats a particular bamboo found only in the Chinese forest. The pandit teas a particular bandarilla found only in the Sinchee foretoken.

The boys go still, look at each other. The pandit…She begins again but never finishes.

At first, the sandstorm seems to sweep over him from the side, the boy at her feet. But, no, it's the long sunset shadow of a man. The boy at her feet is slammed to the ground and killed. It happens so fast she can't see how, only that his head snaps over to one side as his eyes stay open and his pink tongue pokes through sandy lips. There is a whirring sound.

The shadow passes over her quickly, an X-ray over her body, and she feels the belt immediately slacken around her throat. She fingers the belt open and flings it away with a shudder as she gets to her knees, skidding in her sand grave.

She sees that the coyote is strangling the other boy, the boy who held the belt. The coyote has him pinned to the sand with his knees, with his full weight. His arms are bowed and clenched, his red fingers digging into the boy's throat. Above, the boy's throat is black, below the grip it is white, almost translucent. The bike wheel still protrudes from the coyote's back, from between his shoulder blades, spinning and arced to the sky.

•

She rolls the bodies into the scoop. The coyote, still on his knees, starts to tug the jeans the rest of the way off one of the bodies. It pains him. The clear wind at the front edge of the sandstorm has fully reached them now and it spins the wheel on his back, spins it steadily. When she realizes what he is trying to do, she stops him.

No, she tells him. I would rather be naked than wear anything of theirs.

He nods, but even that movement pains him further.

She motions to the wheel. You want me to pull it out?

He tries to say no but the only sound he can make is the *ooooo* through one of the tubes. Phlegm seeps from the end of that tube, a very light trickle of blood from the ragged end of the other. He mimes the way you make an *n*-sound and then the *ooooo* follows. She recognizes the *n*-sound locution from her studies of Saussure. But together it all registers as *newwwww*.

They leave the bodies to be buried by the oncoming sandstorm. Two whirlwinds of sand have already passed over them. Pellets that spin free sting her body. At first, she tries to cover herself with her arms and hands, from the flying grains of sand and from the coyote. But then she decides to let him look. Why not? He is going soon.

She waves her arm over the first line of buildings at the edge of this endless sweep of one-story buildings, solar panels on all the roofs shimmering in the fading light. The lowest, heaviest bar of the sandstorm has almost eclipsed sunset. She waves her arm. Pick one. Pick a place.

She recognizes the *t*-sound he is trying to make, his tongue going up behind his top teeth. But all his breath goes through the top tube protruding from his chest. *T-ooooo*.

Too? She looks at him and his eyes plead. *Tú*, she says. You want me to pick.

As they walk toward the place she chooses—she just counts n+7 over to the right—she tries to gauge his wounds. There is hardly any blood. There is that thin trickle from the one tube and there is a line of wetness on the back of his blue shirt, the same line you get when you ride a bike after a rain. But he is going soon.

They approach the first line of buildings from behind. The backyards are all unkempt and merely fade into the desert. None of the pig-wire fences are intact or complete. They sag with invitation.

She knows he is going because she once saw a quarry dog go this way. It was one of her cousin's favorite pooches, one that never begged but just rested quietly in the shade and was content with whatever scraps were offered. But it took a projectile thrown by a hopper malfunction. A chunk of concrete with re-bar impaled the poor beast in the back. The dog hardly yelped, looked at Equisa and her cousin once as though ashamed, and trotted along the slabs to find the best shade. The chunk of concrete rode its back as if balanced. But Equisa and her cousin knew that it was the re-bar that held it there. No blood flowed. But they knew it was seeping inside. They followed it. It found the shaded entrance to one of the best caves and laid down and died without a whimper.

They bang on the backdoor of the place, figuring that anyone looking like they do should come from the desert side. The coyote must stoop because of the wheel but does his best to wear a calm and respectful expression, as best his battled face can project. He can at least keep his lips softly closed because he breathes through the tubes. The breaths are quick and shallow, rhythmical. Equisa can imagine his heartbeat from the breath-patterns. Recent events leave her in her most sensitive reading mode.

She finds optimism even in the closed door, the shell of the paint hard and smooth against the desert, well-kept, not like the yard. Those behind the door respect the desert, what comes from it, what survives it. This'll work, she tells the coyote.

A woman opens the door. Her hair is half gray, half black, not mixed but in fat streaks. Equisa counts seventeen streaks total and thinks the woman has survived something that many times. She also wonders if she is over-reading, over-reading because she is worked up by recent events. The woman answering the door offers them each more than one glance. She sees worse than this in her life in this building, worse than what stands at her door now. Worse, thinks Equisa, but not more unique—a naked woman accompanied by a kind of centaur, half man, half bicycle. The woman raises an eyebrow, creasing the thin lace of wrinkles on her forehead and temple. Equisa knows she is here alone but doesn't live here alone, not all the time. The workday is ending with the sandstorm and the coming dusk.

I just need clothes, says Equisa, and to help him go. I can pay you if you have a phone.

The woman hands her a phone and Equisa brushes her fingers over the screen, skin-soft, and pays her in advance. She hands the phone back and watches the woman see what she has paid her.

She waves them in and closes the door after watching two dust devils hurled forward by the approaching storm cross her backyard, jump the pig-wire. Equisa scans the room. A husband, a son, and two daughters, all working age, live here, too. Another family of cousins live here sometimes, too, four in number. The building is all one room except for the bath which is behind a door. Four shoji screens fashioned from pig-wire and gauze divide the room. The screens are decorated: two with fresh marigolds, one with a string of lime-fizz bottle caps, one with a garland of tennis balls. The son's nook, marked by the bottle caps garland, has books in it, shelved on cinderblocks and metal planks. The books are not the old, authentic kind. They are contemporary, the kind assembled from elixir and placards. The kind you don't have to read. You just close your eyes, drink the tea, and peek at the pictures on the placards from time to time. But from the outside, the books look just like the old kind. The cinderblocks remind her of the Tijuana quarry.

To keep from reading too much, she shakes her head. She rubs her head, too, and for the first time fingers the uneven brush on her scalp. Because the woman understands Equisa's border Spanish, she knows there is even more family in the North, sending money down, coming sometimes for Christmas, sometimes for Easter.

In the center clearing, a stove, fridge, and table are clumped together around a column of wires and piping that goes straight up to the solar panel on the roof. This woman leads a happy life, a profoundly happy life, and Equisa draws a deep breath, finally a deep and measured breath.

The woman disappears behind a marigold shoji and comes back with some of her daughter's clothes: torn jeans almost the color of milk, tennis shoes, and a Team Mexico soccer shirt, number fourteen.

First things first, the woman says and hands Equisa the clothes. Equisa dresses as the coyote turns away best he can. Every movement pains him. He stoops with his arms hanging still and straight.

Dressed, Equisa turns to the coyote and asks him what he needs. She reads him. He eases himself down on his knees, sits back on his boot heels, finding rest like he did when he was a boy harvesting strawberries in Baja. If he could draw breath through his nose he would even smell them, she thinks, them and the cool salt air of the Guadalupe Valley.

Painfully, he cranes his look up to Equisa and the woman. He elocutes the *b*-sound for English or the *v*-sound for Spanish. Then sounds the *ooooo*. Then he opens his mouth, folds his tongue back against his throat. *K*.

B–oooo–K.

He wants to read a book, Equisa tells the woman. Can he read one of your son's books?

The woman passes her phone to Equisa. Equisa takes the phone, brushes in payment, returns it to the woman. In tiny increments, her cousin's inheritance dwindles.

The woman nods toward her son's bookshelf just visible beyond the lime-fizz shoji. Equisa moves toward the books and looks back for the coyote to follow. But he remains very still in his pose, sitting on his heels, shoulders stooped, arms dangled. The spokes of the bike wheel cut up the evening light slanting through the two front windows. The wheel doesn't spin but rolls softly back-and-forth with his breathing. *T–ooooo,* he tells her. *Tú*.

She begins to choose for him. Most of the son's collection is stuff she doesn't know: sci-fi, horror, fantasy, detective. She thumbs along the covers as the woman puts a kettle of water on the stove and sets an empty mug on the table.

Equisa is just about to quit searching, to just let the coyote read something easy and pleasant before he goes, when her thumb catches Juan Rulfo's *El llano en llamas*. She searches no further, tilts the book from the shelf, checks to see if it's complete. It has five placards and its cut-out holds three teabags and a half-full vial of powder. The son has read it twice, she thinks, not shared it. If he read it once and shared it once, he would not have kept it buried and hidden in his collection. She begins to like the boy.

She brings the Rulfo to the coyote and shows it to him. He nods, barely lifting his chin really.

You know it?

N–ooooo. Newwwww.

Then prepare yourself, she tells him. For something beautiful.

They all wait a moment for the kettle to come to a boil. The woman stands at the stove with grace and pride, holds a tin spoon for stirring and measuring. Twilight fills the room, getting a little brighter because the sandstorm subsides in the evening cool. The sand raised into the sky by the storm now falls in a light rain on the roof. It spitters on the solar panel. Perfect for the Rulfo, thinks Equisa.

She watches the woman prepare the book. She first lays the teabag into the empty mug, presses it to the bottom with the spoon. Then she pours the boiling water lightly into the mug, creating a chortling sound that brings with it a bergamot scent. With two fingers, she lifts and drops the bag three times. She hums a tune as she measures one level spoonful of powder over the tea. Steam from the tea clouds the bottom of the tin spoon. She lets the powder spill into the tea and uses a rhythmical plunging of the bag for the initial mixing before stirring with the spoon.

The coyote's eyes watch the stirring, the only sense of lift about him. The rest of him sags, further and further. The wheel on his back tick-tocks quickly with his shallow breath and shallow pulse.

The woman finds a footstool on which she can serve the book. She sets the tea and placards before him. Equisa lifts his hands to the footstool, laces his fingers into the handle of the mug. She read this way only once in this life, as part of an assignment for one of her archives courses at UNAM. She found it very unsatisfying, a sense of whispers and distant promises, a sense of everything and everyone passing, with spurts of audio, Döppleresque. She saw her friends read this way all the time in the library. Some of them, right before exams, often skipped the tea and booted and mainlined the powder. The library tried to outlaw this the same way they tried to outlaw drinks and snacks, but the students sneaked in candles and kits anyway. Exams were too important. Exams were fatal. Fatal exams.

But Equisa read *El llano en llamas* many times on paper. She brought it, divided in quires, to her cousin's caves in the quarry and they passed the Rulfo stories in pieces back and forth to one another. She broke it into quires and passed them around to others like her because she sensed before most what was about to happen, first the hoarding, then the vanishing. The archivists like her knew first. The readers in their caves realized last. All books on paper would disappear.

The coyote sips the tea with one hand and fingers the placards with the other. The graphics on the first placard show frogs, their sticky round toes gripping cobblestones. Equisa can close her eyes and just about read with him, or so she imagines. *I am sitting by the sewer waiting for the frogs to come out.*

The coyote guzzles the tea even though it must be scalding his throat. He flips and shuffles the placards quickly with numb fingers. His eyelids droop over images. Equisa avoids the images, not wanting to wreck her own visions of Rulfo's stories. She watches the coyote's expressions, can tell when he reaches the fog and ash and morning peals of the sixth story, "At Daybreak." That's the one she hopes for him.

When his expression goes sad, the saddest one, she knows he's reached the thirteenth story: *There was the moon. Facing them. A large red moon that filled their eyes with light and stretched and darkened its shadow over the earth.* That's the one she wants for him.

Maybe he finishes all fifteen, maybe not. His expression never recovers from the thirteenth story. No dogs bark, she says to him. It comes out as both taunt and salve, letting him hear that she knows the Rulfo, too, is with him in it. Her smile is also both taunt and salve, as always, something she can never change. All she can do is reserve it, save it for those moments when both apply.

The coyote doesn't seem able to move. His hand has fallen away from the empty mug. His other hand limply allows the woman to slide the placards free and return the book to its place on her son's shelf, to be read two more times. The coyote sits on his heels, shoulders stooped, arms draped to the footstool, bike wheel barely ticking back and forth above the curve of his spine.

Now what, *Freund*? She tries to sound casual, throwing in the German for him. She tries to accentuate the salve in her smile. Now what can I do for you?

He mimes *t*, then makes the *ooooo*-sound. She interprets too quickly and thinks *tú* again, thinks he wants her to decide for him. Unable to look up, he repeats himself. *t–ooooo*...Then she sees it, crouches lower to see it, another mime at the end. *M*.

t–ooooo–m.

Tomb.

She looks at the woman. Do you have a scrap of tin and a nail?

The woman passes her phone to Equisa and goes to fetch the items. She returns from behind one of the marigold shojis with three pieces of tin cut into different shapes: heart, circle, jackal head. Equisa chooses the jackal.

Your name? she asks the coyote.

He can only gaze, his eyelids almost lulled shut. She must read, read him, read everything she can for him. This understanding, in all that has happened, is what breaks her. It's what makes her give up inside, surrender, resign herself as prisoner, imprisoned insurgent. She cries. She is crying for herself—and for her cousin a little. But it's okay because to the others in the room it looks as if she cries for the coyote.

She draws back a sob and begins. Z, she thinks, that is the impression, everything about him. His teeth, his body, the way he moves, rests, slashing from side to side, traveling this way then the other.

Zapata, she guesses, but with that smile, taunt and salve. Then Zurillo, Lopez, Gomez, Mendez...Then she recalls the German accent and says, Guzman.

She sees the coyote's eyelids lift, hears an extra hollow gasp from his tube. He shapes his lips into a circle. Her studies of Saussure let her know that this is one of those locutions found always and everywhere. In Spanish, J, in English, H. Our first sound, as we exhale that first breath that commits us to life.

He makes one final *ooooo*-sound through his tube. From that she gets Julio.

Julio Guzman, she says.

The coyote opens his eyes wide as he can. He wants to hear it again.

Julio Guzman. She speaks it carefully, doesn't smile. Julio Guzman.

With hammer and nail she punches the coyote's name into the piece of tin shaped like a jackal head.

Equisa can't walk far even though the woman helps set the coyote piggy-back, hooking one bike tube over a shoulder, lacing his arms below her neck, tucking his shins over her hips. Equisa can feel his jaw pressing the top of her scalp. She carries the load into the desert, stomping forward with momentum, envisioning it as one long stumble and fall. She just wants to get clear of the building lights, to get around the first finger of rocks, find a crease for the body.

The coyote's neck presses her ear and his pulse is a bird heart flicking against death. She wants to get clear of the building lights, clear of any dog barks, clear into only the howls of coyotes. She understands that he wants this, this man who spends his life taking others to what they needed, taking what was needed to others, never taking himself anywhere.

I read the scrap, she says to him as she lurches over the

sand. Maybe that's what gets you killed. Maybe someone saw. That woman on the bus. The one you paid. She was looking for anything. Or maybe we were doomed from the start. Maybe they followed me, maybe you. But I want you to know: I read what you brought to me. And I will finish it. All of it.

A rattling sounds from one of the tubes. She doesn't know what it is, what it means.

Remember in the Rulfo story? The moon? It appeared in different colors. Red, orange, blue. We have a white moon. You can't look up, but you see its light on the sand. It's white, like paper.

You'll hear the coyotes howl. Soon you'll hear them howl.

She makes it around the first finger of stone, around the end, and trudges along the base of its slope until she is clear of the lights. Her shadow on the sand is now cast only by the moon. Together, her form, the coyote's, and the half-bike stuck into his back cast a distinct silhouette on the white desert, a kind of letter from a lost alphabet, a petroglyph, from when letters were asked to do too much.

The collapse is easier than she anticipates. Eyeing her shadow, she slows her pace but doesn't stop. She buckles one knee forward and slides into the sand, sloughing the coyote off to the side. Without wait or rest she drags him by the shoulders into a wedge of stone, making sure there's no pressure on the bike wheel. In recline, he fits neatly into the wedge.

She doesn't know how she will cover him when the time comes. To the moon, which he can see now if he can still see, she holds the tin jackal head with his name punched through it. His name is many points of light on the eclipse. She then sets the tin marker on the front end of the wedge and in the coyote's mind it must be still shining that way, throwing light out of the rock.

Free of his weight, she feels light enough to float, fearfully light. A breeze could come and toss her over the ridge. She rests in the sand and counts stones small enough for her to carry, near enough.

She revisits the break within herself. She knows when she first cries that this moment will present itself. There are no tears in this cry. She cries in words, covers him first in words before the stones.

I have three letters, she tells him, the end-fragment of a word: *ure*. Don't think that's not enough. That's what makes me sad, that's what brings this breaking feeling inside me, starting at the level of my heart, then rising, then falling. It doesn't break me to think that they are all I have, they are all that's left. It breaks me to know those letters are enough. Enough for me to read everything. For me to find the rest. For me to tell you everything.

Fifteen

I CLOSED THE BOOK and flipped it toward the foot of the bed where it landed in the sheet valley between us. The long read left me thirsty and I started to rise in order to get us some water. Marisa pulled me back down and kissed me, fit her body to mine. Bracing her hand to my nape, she held the kiss, a clean mineral taste on her tongue.

She left the bed. Naked, she carried the reading lamp back to its corner. The hooded light bobbed at her side and cast her half in shadow, her giant silhouette moving across the wall. Climbing the steps of Calafia had leaned her out more than usual and I wondered how it might be for us to grow old, not together, but knowing the other, seeing the other like this.

The reading seemed to have relaxed her attitude toward me, given her enough to work with in terms of me explaining myself, whatever fugue she sensed from me. She moved like someone putting a room in order. After returning the lamp, to my surprise, she exited the doorway to the loading bay. Her bare feet pecked lightly on the concrete floor.

She called in gentle worry from the darkness. "Jack, where's the cart?"

"In front of the burn bin." I got up and started to dress, but then wondered if she wanted us to walk around naked, free ourselves.

"No. It's gone."

I pulled on my pants and hustled to the doorway.

Marisa was standing in front of the bin, shining her phone light into the empty space where the pull-cart should have been.

"And I smell smoke."

•

We hiked the narrow cart path toward Cuervo. The cover of live oak and jojoba deepened the night with heavy shadows and a tar smell. I could have navigated the route eyes closed, but Marisa used her light to quicken our pace. Her work heels clicked against the asphalt.

As we neared the plateau, I whispered for her to remove her shoes and cut the light. We could see the incinerator's glow above the scrub and rocky outcrop. A steady wind sound carried over the mountainside like an echo of the sea. Cuervo was in full burn.

I placed my hand on Marisa's arm. "Don't stop her," I whispered. "Don't confront her."

"Her? You know who it is?"

"Catalina's the only one who can get it to burn like that. To get it going like that."

When we reached the plateau, we kept ourselves hidden behind the first line of boulders. Cuervo's belly put forth a pale hot light. The entire flat looked like a moon-landing, the ground struck white, all shadows black and thrown outward. The cart was parked facing the blackness beyond the ledge. Hitched to it was a flatbed trailer, something I had not seen before. On it were three large book cartons, with room for five more.

Cat, still dressed for work, stood in front of Cuervo's open belly. Hands on hips and much of her hair come loose from its bun, she appeared done with a fight.

Marisa and I looked to one another, a relief from the flame light, then watched as Cat opened one of the remaining cartons and pulled out an armful of books. She tossed the whole into the flames. One volume fell free. She picked it up, considered it for a moment, almost opened it, then flipped it in with the others. Cuervo's wind increased with the added fuel. The smoke from his wing tips obscured the stars.

Marisa rested a calming hand on my back. We watched Catalina toss the rest of the carton's holdings into the flames, followed by the box itself. She reassumed her stance, letting the incinerator reach full bore. She became a sliver against the blinding push of light and I feared she might catch fire. Her expression was a mix of resolve and surrender, as though she shared my fear.

•

Along our return to Calafia, we stopped at Brigadoons to stand above the ocean, a way of cooling ourselves. Marisa stood back and one step away. The tide had come in and the surf was hammering the cliff. In the blackness below, everything was sound until the biggest waves shot geysers into the night sky, their heavy mist drifting over us.

I reached back, held my hand out for her. Marisa let me stay like that for a moment before she stepped into my reach, pushed her shoulder to mine.

"Are you going to tell her?"

"Not unless I have to."

"What would make you have to?"

"I don't know. Maybe I'd have to warn her. Maybe it might start to bother me, scare me."

Marisa pulled me closer. "Maybe you'd have to blackmail her."

The sound of a very heavy wave rolled toward us. I moved my hand to her hip and braced myself against her form. Marisa lifted her chin and closed her eyes. At first there was silence, as though the wave had lipped out and failed to form. Then I felt it. That silent drop before the crash, one heartbeat. The wave crashed high against the cliff, the roar loud enough to echo off the hillsides overlooking Ensenada. It sent three geysers into the stars.

Marisa and I didn't bother to run. We huddled and let the fall of seawater pummel us, soak us. We clutched each other. Her fingers gripped my back. The water kept falling. When I moved to kiss her, she turned her lips away and offered only her cheek. And I knew that she would have to do that but hoped anyway. Hoped that time and consequence could vanish within the expanse of a wave's break.

•

WE STOOD SOAKED IN our work clothes. Marisa held her shoulders together and gazed at the dark hills above Ensenada. I loosened my tie and collar and let the water seep over my chest. There were other incinerators and burn piles glowing along the line of hills and I could tell that she was trying to figure which one was Cuervo.

"It's the second one from the left," I said.

She locked onto that one and nodded. "What are the others burning?"

"I don't look at them that way," I said. "I try to wonder what they're making or clearing or preserving. Night fires are the end of a day's work."

She shivered. I stepped close but did not hold her, waited to see. She slid into me and I wrapped my arm around her shoulders, gave her what warmth I could.

"Would you be doing the same thing?" she asked. "If you had taken her position? Back when."

"I can't say that I wouldn't."

Sixteen

THE WAVE HAD SHOVED me to the depths. Already ten feet under, the full stretch of my leash, I would have plunged to the very bottom, where it was dark and milled with sand. The buoyancy of my longboard was saving me, keeping me tied to the air. I climbed the leash, hand over hand, my lungs bursting. The surface foam made the morning sun appear brighter. I raced against the next wave.

I broke the surface just in time to release my lungs and gather a new breath before the oncoming wave pounded me back under. Then it yanked my board toward shore, pulling me along like tattered kelp. To struggle would have been a mistake. I let the ride skim me to the surface where I was able to take in shallow, salty gasps.

Flaco glided into the breakwater to check on me. I stood hunched in the waist-deep shallows as he eased off his board and placed a hand to the small of my back.

"What the hell are you doing, Jack?"

I tried to laugh, but it came out as a watery cough.

"I don't want to be old, Flaco."

"You couldn't ride these waves young, Jack."

We let the rollers slap us toward shore. We unleashed and our boards scooted in ahead of us. With his long legs, Flaco strode the breakwater with ease, metallic in his wetsuit. I floated a bit, crawled, until I felt my breath and strength returning. Sunrise glittered yellow along the tips of the black cliffs.

Onshore he pretended to be as beat as I was. We knelt in the sand, suits peeled down to our waists. Flaco measured the swells. I looked farther to the span of ocean between breakers and horizon. This was one of the best times to spot grays, with the slant of sunrise coming from behind you, the water glassy before the wind rose with the day's heat.

A spout, about a half-mile offshore, caught the morning sun. The whale's bow followed, curling above the surface. Another spout, just behind, indicated a pod. I pointed to let Flaco know. I looked away to re-set my vision, saw him smile as he spotted the whales. We watched a series of spouts, bows, and flukes break the surface.

"A pod of three," said Flaco. "Maybe four, yeah?"

This was good for my eyes, the opposite of reading, the opposite of the day ahead of me. I was taking in an ocean, using full span, my focus on the feathery spouts, my peripheral gathering context. My imagination could go anywhere—to memory, to the future, to the underwater life of these gray whales—and I would still be able to comprehend what I was seeing. Words on a page were more anchoring, the imagination linked and guided and challenged, freed to some extent, but if it strayed too far comprehension would be lost. You'd have to read the words again.

"I need to go to the Tijuana storage yards. Where all those shipping bins are."

Flaco kept his eyes on the whale pod, squinted. "You've never once invited me for a drink. Taken me to that fancy place on the cliffs where we would be treated like kings." He turned to me. "And now you need me to take you to the yards."

"I don't need you. It would just go a lot better if you were there. I'm guessing."

"You're guessing by what?"

"By you."

"You understand the insult."

"I do."

He watched one of the riders take the first wave of a set. We could both see that he should have waited. The set had a nice build to it, the first two waves mere harbingers.

"There's a drink in it for you," I said. "At Calafia. Afterward. We'll have margaritas and spot whales until the light is gone."

I was pressing the insult, figuring Flaco might admire my honesty in letting him know what I thought of him. And all I really thought of him was as a person who made money in some kind of unconventional manner. In Baja. Which automatically connected one to Tijuana, to its ins and outs, its formal expression, its informal truth.

"I'll do it," he said. "But not while the surf's this good."

•

As USUAL, I DRESSED for work without showering. It felt especially good this morning to wrap myself in shirt and tie with the salt prickle on my skin, sand in my hair, a tidal scent on my neck and hands. I liked my deal with Flaco. The Pacific swell would determine when I would go to see our holdings in the Tijuana bins, if it was to be before or after my official tour up north with Valeria. It seemed the proper Baja way of doing things.

I suppose I shared Nietzsche's *Amor fati*, mainly because it embraced fatalism rather than merely accepting it, asked us to recognize fate, to discover love in the unassailable. I do think Frederich would have done better in life if he had sought recuperation in Baja rather than Turin. I regretted not kissing Marisa twenty-eight years ago in the place of the hummingbirds. I sometimes wondered if I had kissed her, if she would have then loved me that much more, enough to have stayed with me when I chose not to accept San Diego, to stay at the EPL.

When I arrived for work, Cisco was there between the bougainvillea with his bucket and broom. We exchanged Spanish good mornings. He paused in his sweeping. Did he have something to say or was he sensing that I had something to say? After yesterday's events, fate was that palpable to me, there to acknowledge, there to love, there to embrace in the smallest of life's movements.

I thought to ask him how many books were in the EPL when it first started. I wondered what was the most beautiful book he had ever held in his hands or which one he had read the most times. He offered me that Picasso stare, a lulling gaze as he held his broom above the bucket.

"She's already here," he said.

"Catalina?"

"No," he replied. "The other one."

An alligator lizard scampered across the terracotta, paused at the edge of the walkway, then rustled into the papery duff of the bougainvillea. I inhaled the warm stone air of Cisco's work. He returned to his sweeping.

The front doors were closed but unlocked. I opened both and set their stops. The warmer outside air rushed in behind me. Valeria sat within the circle desk, watching me in a deliberate manner that let me know she had been staring all along. She didn't speak until I neared the circle.

"It's so easy for us to sin," she said.

I had no intention of stopping on my way to the reading room. I paused and gave her a confused look.

"Librarians, I mean." She tapped a pencil against her chin. "The sins of a librarian are easy. Easy to do, easy to forget."

I looked back to the wide-open doorway, then to her. "The

outside air here isn't bad. It's the right temperature and it's not too humid, not too dry. It's 72 outside and the humidity is 38. I'm not as careless and sinful as I seem."

Like a patron, I leaned on the desk.

"Do you know those numbers for surfing?" she asked. "Or for the books."

I leaned closer to see what she was doing. Cat had left us our four cartons for the day, her final chore last night before heading up the hill to burn eight more. On top of one of the cartons was the copy of *Equisa*.

She noticed me eyeing the book.

"Found it in the basement apartment," she said. "Someone had sex in that room last night."

She offered me *Equisa*. "Yours?"

"You can put it in the chute." I headed for the reading room.

"Casanova was a librarian, you know." She tapped with her pencil. This time her lips. "For thirteen years."

"So was Mao."

She had to talk louder as I strode toward the reading room archway. Her voice echoed throughout the foyer. "So was Batgirl."

•

THE MORNING BREEZE WAS filling the reading room. I gathered books left on the tables, straightened the lamps. Valeria was right. It was a bit of a sin to let in the outside air, as perfect as it may have seemed in terms of temperature and humidity. Along with the refreshing Baja air, it was also bringing in millions of spores, fungi and yeasts that might feed on paper, paste, cloth, even ink. Rare books under glass in controlled environments—to me and others—were entombed volumes. Some librarians believed the way to keep the holdings alive was to keep them as active as possible, to allow them to interact with the environment.

And the truth was, people represented the greatest threat. Our touch and our breath and the slough from our bodies brought the worst contaminants. If you considered books mere objects, then you had to know they decayed. If you were more romantic and revered them as life, then you had to know that they died.

Being a librarian was to be an understanding hypocrite. It was a matter of forever searching for the least sin within an existence defined by an endless series of sins. I lifted myself onto one of the reading tables and lay back. This was the best way to take in the vertical wonder of the reading room. The book-lined walls swept upward, two stories high. The light from the cupola became a pulling light, drawing the holdings into it. The high thin windows fed into this effect. I spread my arms, dangled my feet over the table ledge.

"I dropped your book into the chute. As ordered."

Valeria's quiet voice feathered its way into my thoughts. I wasn't sure she was there. Upon seeing her, I sat up but remained atop the table. I checked the overhead clock and told her that one of us should be manning the front desk.

"We have a moment," she replied. "Did you look up the author?"

I rubbed my eyes as though waking. "J.B. D'Acquisto? Why would I do that?"

"He's a teacher at a little college way up in Minnesota. He probably used *Equisa* to get the job."

"Good for him."

"I don't know," she said. "It's sad. He clearly loves Mexico. Needs to be there."

She hoisted herself up to sit next to me, her shoulder

bouncing off mine. I inched away, but when I looked to her I still felt too close, would not have wanted Cisco to see us.

"You *read* it?"

"Some." She cocked her head thoughtfully. "It's weird."

"So you tossed it."

"No." She exaggerated the word with her lips. "*You* tossed it."

"Okay, fine." I straightened my legs, looked at my shoes. "*Would* you have tossed it?"

"That's impossible for me to answer. My system relies on going in unencumbered. The volume is just an object. Finding it like that on a bed made it a book. Especially a bed like *that*."

I dropped my feet, let them dangle. We were like kids on the end of a dock. "What the hell were you doing down there anyway?"

"Oh," she replied. "I pass through every room first thing. Top to bottom. As trained. I paged through some of Cat's sketches in the conservation room. She's pretty good."

"You're quite the snoop."

"I'm here to learn, right? Besides, it's not a house. It's a public library."

I eyed the clock. We were two minutes from opening.

"Who was in the bed with you?" She was watching the clock, too. "Not Cat, I know. Though a lot of her sketches have you in them. Or things related to you. Like the floating books."

"Is it a sin," I asked her. "To have sex in a library?"

She firmed her lips into a thoughtful frown. "It's probably good for the old books. You know? An act of reproduction and all. Sinful as it may have been."

•

SHE LEFT ME ALONE as the clock softly struck nine. Before

strolling away to man the front desk, she left me with our appointment notice to tour the San Diego annex. I saw that the building was a converted hangar somewhere toward the desert. This Sunday, on what was supposed to be my day off, I would be in an arid, abandoned place, being shown one particular fate for books. I pulled the knot of my tie in order to release the tang of the ocean clinging to my chest.

Seventeen

I SWITCHED MORNING DUTIES with Cisco, taking over the re-stacking carts. I did not want to sit in the circle desk with Valeria and the assessment cartons. I knew Catalina was burning eight cartons, then leaving us our usual four. How random was Cat's approach? Had she learned to somehow tell which boxes were most fit for the fire? How long had she been doing this? How well did I trust her discretion? I had admitted to Marisa that I might have done the same thing. Without much thought, I almost always told Marisa the truth.

I began in the third-floor stacks, as far away from the front desk as possible. Re-stacking was the one duty that remained the same after the digital age gained dominance. We lined the books on the wooden carts according to their return positions on the shelves, a system perfected by twelfth-century monks who had to navigate literary labyrinths using only memory, mentorship, and candlelight. We used our digital catalogue to load the carts, but after that it was just us and the books.

The third-floor stacks had portal windows at the end of each aisle and from them you could see the Pacific. From the ones along the east wall, you could see the tile roof of the reading room and the surrounding chaparral. A seagull, looking lost, might cross this particular vista. I worked from one view to the other, parking the cart and walking the aisles with an armful of re-stacks.

If I reached an aisle that had no re-stacks, I walked it anyway, looking for books abandoned on open ends, on top, or on the floor. I tightened the shelves, evened the lines.

Around twenty books into the first cartload, I came across a sheet of paper tucked between pages. I figured it to be a note Cisco left for himself, maybe something to remind him to take a break. The paper was a thick parchment and on it was a hand-written Neruda poem, "I Like for You to Be Still." One side featured the original Spanish, the other the English translation. I saw right away how different the translation was from the original. Each of the three stanzas began with the same line, the title, but then played in a different way with what it might mean to *like* and *to be still.* The second stanza I read twice, in each language.

I like for you to be still
And you seem far away
It sounds as though you are lamenting
A butterfly cooing like a dove
And you hear me from far away
And my voice does not reach you
Let me come to be still in your silence
And let me talk to you with your silence
That is bright as a lamp
Simple, as a ring
You are like the night
With its stillness and constellations
Your silence is that of a star
As remote and candid

But in Spanish, the poem was not the same poem. In Spanish, the title was "*Me gustas cuando callas,*" something more along the lines of "I like when you shut up." And once that was changed, the rest of the poem was refracted. And I imagined Cisco standing about where I was, flipping the page over and back, studying the English reflection of this Spanish poem, finding in that an entirely new poem, one shimmering between the two.

I set the page aside, reminding myself to return it to Cisco.

On the first Sunday of every month, I went to Cisco's house for afternoon beer. An American librarian could live pretty well in Baja. Cisco had a stucco bungalow overlooking San Miguel Bay. Sometimes we watched soccer, but most times we sat on the front porch, watched the sea, and listened to music. He would set out a bowl of potato chips and a plate of lime wedges.

A low stucco wall enclosed the porch. Cisco decorated it with clay pots holding barrel cactus and jade plants. Horned toads would sun themselves on the tile, wary of the occasional gull shadow. Cisco squeezed lime onto his chips, then rimmed the tip of his beer bottle with the pulp.

He had lived alone all of his adult life, almost all of it in that same house. At twenty-five, newly degreed from Wayne State, he started working as a librarian at the EPL, where he has been for forty-five years. He has walked all of the Baja coastline, both the Sea of Cortez side and the Pacific shore. There are long silences during my Sunday visits, filled by the surf and the radio's low volume ranchera. When we do speak, we talk of books and the Baja coast and some of its chaparral flora and fauna. He asks me about the libraries I have visited around the world. He especially likes to ask me about the very small ones that have a sea view, such as the one in Oban. He has told me many times that I will end up there, protecting the library's small collection against the Scottish mist.

Two patrons came and left the third-floor stacks, quickly finding their borrows, not browsing. I was about two-thirds done with my first cart when I came upon another page of that same kind of parchment tucked between books. Handwritten on it was a passage from Lewis Thomas' *The Medusa and the Snail.* I read the last paragraph twice:

> The thought of these creatures gives me an odd feeling. They do not remind me of anything, really. I've never heard of such a cycle before. They are bizarre, that's it, unique. And at the same time, like a vaguely remembered dream, they remind me of the whole earth at once. I cannot get my mind to stay still and think it through.

I was struck by the connections between the notes. Both the Neruda poem and this passage were driven by a quest for stillness. And both centered on a tenuous duality, a plea for union amid separation. What kind of mind could access these two works readily enough to scribble them down as a day's meditations? These two very disparate works, one by a Chilean poet, the other by an American physician?

Again, I stood where Cisco would have been standing between the stacks and paused to hold this parchment with two hands. I studied the handwriting. It was careful, each letter deliberately scribed, almost drawn.

Catalina. She was leaving these for Cisco. I recalled the last time I had switched cart duties with Cisco and figured Cat could have only started leaving these pages within the last month. Were these more for her than for him?

Catalina and I began working at the EPL seventeen years ago. She was thirty, I thirty-four. Cisco was our mentor, having already been here twenty-eight years. Cisco had started forgetting our names one year ago. These numbers meant nothing, really. They were vain attempts to get my mind to stay still and think it through.

Eighteen

Fifteen years ago, Catalina and I visited the Landmark Law Library at the University of Michigan. We were sent there. Cat travelled with her partner at the time, an engineer named Roger who loved to fish and golf and read early Hemingway stories. Roger enjoyed that summer week so thoroughly that he ended up moving there. The only time I ran into Cat during that trip—aside from our required tours and panels—was during our off-hours visits to the Landmark reading room.

Three Oban public libraries could fit into that reading room. It was the classic cathedral-style reading room, a single hall three stories high, vaulted ceiling, elegiac leaded windows. It was lined with long reading tables, lit by reading lamps and chandeliers suspended on chains. It contained no books.

Cat found me there on our first free morning. Roger was fly-fishing somewhere on the Huron River. I was pining for the Pacific. She wore a green sleeveless dress, her reading glasses hanging as necklace. She appeared more exotic than usual in that setting and I imagined her as the safari hunter's wife, abandoned for big game.

She offered me an embarrassed smile.

"Hey," I said. "I'm here, too."

"You know what they didn't mention?" she asked. "On the tour, I mean. They didn't tell us that there are no books."

I nodded.

"You came here because of that," she said.

There were maybe twenty students scattered among the

many tables, but the vastness made it still seem empty, left us feeling alone together.

"Imagine how nice our job would be." She stepped closer, fresh cigarettes.

We spent the next hour reading across from each other at the end of a table. She was reading Howard Norman's *The Bird Artist* and I a novel Marisa had bought for me specifically for this trip, an out-of-print edition of Handke's *The Left-Handed Woman*. Occasionally we would look up from our books, to take in the view and to glance at the other. We'd smile whenever we caught each other.

I wanted to ask her what exactly she meant by how nice our job would be. I wanted to ask her how a guy could leave someone who looked like her to go catch a fish in a river. But I never asked either question. At the end of the hour we walked together to the scheduled group coffee. Two days later, we met again in the Landmark reading room and exchanged novels. I liked hers best and she preferred mine.

•

AFTER I FINISHED RE-STACKING all the morning carts, I went to the basement to find Catalina on break. I was hoping to catch her outside the loading door, smoking. But she was already sketching in the conservation room.

"Not again," she said without looking up from her pad.

I entered the room anyway. "I switched duties with Cisco this morning."

She nodded, kept sketching. Her pencil sounded like a tiny version of Cisco's broom.

"So, you found the notes. Did you read them?"

I moved close to see what she was drawing. She was working on a series of studies of Cuervo, her page covered with various details and angles of the incinerator—chimneys in the upper corners, side views in the center, the burners and the belly-flap in the lower corners.

"How could I not?" I asked.

"You have a way of delaying such things, Jack."

"I liked them."

"Maybe they were for you," she replied. "Maybe they were for me."

"Either way," I said. "Why?"

She paused mid-stroke, keeping her pencil slanted to the paper. A lock of hair swung loose over her ear, the image a remnant from last night, her stance between fire and books.

"You question my methods as head librarian of the EPL?"

"Never," I replied.

"But always, too," she said. "Indirectly."

"It's part of my job."

"I hate that you do it so well."

She leaned back from the studies and offered them, spreading her arms, pencil crooked in fingers. "What do you think?"

"Why are they so dark? You've shaded them so heavily. He looks scorched."

"It's night," she replied. She looked at me frankly. "Ever wonder how he looks at night?"

"Asleep or awake?"

"Feeding," she said. Her eyes were black, sharp, leveled.

She set down her pencil and centered the pad on the table. She cleaned her hands with a soft looking cloth smudged with charcoal.

"Come share a cigarette with me."

•

SHE HIT THE SWITCH to the loading bay door. We stood side by side as the corrugated steel rattled upward and I thought of us as space travelers, off to a new destination, either at the beginning or end of the movie. The outside air rushed by us, corrupting the distilled atmosphere of the library. We could smell heated stone from the hillside and a faint trace of salt mist.

She lit a cigarette and passed it to me. I took two draws, then let her have the rest. We spoke of Cisco, of our Sunday visits with him. Hers were the second Sunday of the month. She claimed these were debriefings, following my visits. I told her that I always looked forward to those afternoons with Cisco. She told me that he lets us know that it's okay to end up living alone, that we, as librarians, were destined for it.

Nineteen

IN THE DREAM I want to have, Cuervo pulls himself free of the mountainside and walks the Earth, inhaling books, shooting their ashes into the sky. Or he flies, his tin wings creaking, his belly flap opening above the next library. Instead, I dreamed of Equisa as I napped on the beach during my lunch break. Brigadoons was empty, the surf blown out and ragged. Its whoosh and rhythm lulled itself into my sleep, became the sound of the sandstorm that drove Equisa and the wounded coyote to seek cover. Sometimes I was the coyote in the dream, dying and unable to speak. But I was able to read the way he read in the novel, drinking a tea while gazing at wooden panels that depicted the main scenes, the books getting inside me without the awkward need for words, for paper and ink.

Marisa wakened me, brushing a wet kelp leaf along my jaw. She knelt over me, blocking the sun. I had started my nap in the shade of the rocks. Now the breakwater swooped close, the shadows retracted, the tide approaching.

"Lucky I showed," she said. "If the sun didn't get you, the sea would have."

Above me, she was half-silhouette, the afternoon sun haloing her head and shoulders. Still, I could see her amused expression, and I could tell she had cut her hair this morning. It was very short again, almost the way she had it when we first met.

I reached to feel the brush along her nape.

"Did you buy a motorcycle?"

"Just the opposite," she replied. "I'm letting the gray take over."

I stirred my fingers in her forelock, the longest part of her cut. She leaned into my hand, then flipped the lock free of her eyes.

"It's about a third," she said. "If that's what you're looking for."

"I didn't even know you were dyeing it."

"Mmm. For about five years now."

I gathered myself into a kneel and offered her a place on my towel. "I want to grow a beard." I rubbed my chin. "But it's so gray."

"You'd look good."

"I'd have to buy a metal detector and a pair of Speedos."

She dropped two brown bags between us. "I brought lunch."

"How did you find me?"

"Cat. I showed up at the desk. She guessed." Marisa bowed her head, sat back on her heels. "It's still strange for me, after all these years, to watch the two of you. How you work together. It's like you think the guesses you make about each other are somehow better than what's real. And you can both just leave it at that."

"We talked." I looked at the breakwater's churn, the blown-out surf beyond.

She shook her head and held her hands to the shore, as if staving off the waves. "I don't care. Just don't do it with me."

"Okay." I scooped a handful of sand and let it hourglass into a pyramid. "I love you, Marisa. I never stopped loving you. And I feel very alone in that. When I'm not with you, which is almost all the time. That's how I go about my life. Trying to find solace in that."

"I'm sorry," she replied.

"Don't apologize. You were right. We are best like this."

She laughed softly. "A Baja relationship."

"Sure," I said. "Let's call it that."

We looked at the two unopened lunch bags. She picked up hers and returned it to her satchel. Inside the satchel, I spotted the copy of *Equisa.* I motioned to the book.

"Did you snitch that from the burn bin?"

She thumbed the cover, exposing more. "It wasn't in the bin. It was on the bed. Where we left it last night. I went there to find you and there it was, neatly on the pillow. I was going to read more of it, maybe on the beach, maybe with you. You put it in the *chute*?"

"Valeria did."

"The new one." Marisa rubbed her neck, feeling her new cut. "She's an odd bird. A pretty bird."

"You spoke?"

"She found me in the basement. Told me you were already on break. Then she told me about the morning you were having."

"The morning I was having?"

Marisa shrugged. "Like I said. An odd bird. She told me—us actually. By that time Catalina had found us. She told us you were like a guy underwater, trying to tug yourself to the surface. But not too fast."

"We talked about nothing. About Casanova and Bat Girl," I replied. "She doesn't even know me," I replied.

"You're not that hard to know, Jack." She offered me the book.

I shook my head and waved it away.

"Read a bit more," she said. "Before you burn it. Read the part about Tolan's theory of erasure."

I took the book, looked at it, considered her.

She shrugged. "I read some more sitting on the bed, kind of waiting for you."

She shoved the lunch bag at me, too. “Eat. Read. Tamales from that place you like. And some papaya and mango. How you like them, cubed, with a lime for squeezing.”

“Tolan’s theory of erasure?” I asked.

Twenty

MARISA LEFT. I TUCKED myself into some shade, back against the base of the cliff, and read. I ate the papaya and mango cubes, using a toothpick so as not to get the pages sticky. After leaving Equisa alone, kneeling by the coyote's makeshift grave, the novel went back in time as she recalls how she first came to know her cousin, the one whose ashes she spread over the volcano at the story's opening. The reader discovers more about Equisa's work and life, and more about the cousin. Like Equisa, he is a reading savant, one who can still read from paper. But instead of being an archivist or scholar, he works as a hopper in Tijuana, a person who operates these powerful and dangerous machines that render urban detritus into re-usable material. Cities are disappearing center outward as forms of work, communication, and exchange become progressively digital, less corporeal. But her Cousin X still works with his hands and body. It's a job and lifestyle that allows him to read the scraps of books he finds among the rubble.

I read twelve pages. With the mango and papaya, it took me twenty-four minutes. That had always been my reading pace, eating or not. Two minutes per page. There were a lot of references to Juan Rulfo's *El Llano en Llamas* and Julio Cortázar's *Hopscotch*. Ten years earlier, Equisa was on the run, escaping from circumstances similar to the ones involving the coyote and his scrap of paper:

> She remembers the first time she barely escapes death because of work, because she had to deal with coyotes

who smuggled the past into the present. She carries a disintegrating edition of Cortázar's *Rayuela*, its hopscotch chapters beginning to break free of their crumbling binding. Maybe like the author wanted anyway, she thinks as she emerges from the sand, cradling what's left of the volume. This grave she digs for herself, buries herself within, a place to hide as the vans roll above, nearly crushing her, angry voices grinding above the gears. But they avoid her grave because she takes care to mark it, hangs a long lock of her hair from one end of the makeshift cross. Beneath the Baja sand, she breathes through the tube of an antique pen long empty of its ink.

She lets the sand fall from her clothes after she gets free of her grave and continues to cradle the book, lets herself believe that she has won for now. She wonders if the coyote who brought her the dying book managed to escape as well, wonders what he had up *his* sleeve.

As planned, she takes refuge in a big family wedding in Tijuana. She finds the tuxedo she had hidden for herself in the downtown Cultural Center where the reception was to be held.

It's a sprawling affair and the expanse of the Center, its floor lights stretching everyone into half-shadows, is just big enough. Anyone slightly connected to either family is invited. They fill the ground floor with their music and dancing, escape in clusters into the gardens to catch their breath, and spill into the blockaded streets of Plaza del Rio to see if the rest of the world can survive their revelry. It makes sense that Equisa and her cousin finally meet. They are the two notorious members of the extended family. She is an archivist, someone who can still read from paper, who has all the rumored curses and powers associated with that activity. Most steer clear of her, even the men—except maybe those who will try to screw anything that looks good, monster or not.

Hoppers like her cousin are notorious for living indulgent, carefree lives, musketeers who must experience who and what they can before they are suddenly killed or maimed by the machines that make them rich. Along with the good salaries they have free nights and weekends. They send money north and south, gaining kinship reverence so they can sin as much as they want. There are not many of them. Equisa learns later that a dozen others work the Tijuana quarry with her cousin. There are maybe a hundred or so quarries in all of Mexico, but more blooming with every passing year and every passing city.

With her hair up and her tux perfectly tailored, she feels confident in her masquerade, but is nonetheless ready to leave. She stands near the main table where the bride's family throws glances and is clearly talking about her. She endures this as expected ritual, that this is the last table on her list of tables to which she is expected to show herself, the family *bruja*. She pretends to be finishing a glass of champagne. Then the two cousins see each other. They stare for longer than twenty seconds. Seeing someone else get watched for twenty seconds, it doesn't seem so long. When it is you in the gaze, it feels a very long time. But it is expected from her, this curse. Why, she wonders, would a hopper return her stare, hold it for as long she could? How?

They know one another's name, so the introduction is easy. She calls his first. Almost immediately they dispose of these given names and agree on Cousin X, Equisa/Equis. They lightly grasp hands and formally kiss cheeks. A puff of air rises from inside his starched collar, the sweet scent of a book crease. Or does she imagine that one?

She expects powder and gin, telltale signs of a hopper's life. You don't smell like a hopper, she tells him.

I never go to clubs, he says. I live a monkish life, navigating between my little downtown flat and my quarry caves.

She draws back but still grasps his fingers. To the bride's table it must appear they are about to dance. You read books, she says in English, in a low whisper.

Everyone reads books, he replies.

She gets another angle on him, her neck stretched over, head atilt. You know what I mean.

The bride's table, in furtive glances, get the show they want. The cousins perfect the wedding party for them, no doubt, the parry between the archivist and the hopper, the devout and the lout. But if the table could look at one thing for more than twenty seconds, if they could read, they would see that he perhaps was more devout than she.

Mi prima, he whispers back to her. I do know what you mean. But how can you tell?

The bend of your elbow, she whispers. As you took hold of my fingers. You hold me as a book, holding still, your thumb in the crease of my palm. You're accustomed to the delicacy of paper. You, a hopper, used to handling the roughest and heaviest materials.

They step farther away from the bride's table, more to the edge of the dancing, a kind of waltz about them, still in view. The music is ranchera, the accordion muted enough, playing long notes instead of so many of those quick-step ones. They can easily hear one another, but list on the apron of the dancing, in view of the tables yet out of earshot.

And here is when she asks him more than once why he doesn't go to university. He evades the real answer several times, telling her about how he prefers his caves, that he gets enough on his own, even finds a book or pieces of books in the rubble of the quarry. But there is no hope of fooling her. She reads all of him. So, she asks until he speaks the truth.

He tells her that he once found some quires and loose pages of a book, a novel. It had no author but it was titled *The Last Cronopio*. It looked as though it was translated from Spanish because some of the idioms were off and some of the sentences were enjambed. It was beautiful and poetic and he could tell the translator never wanted to sacrifice the language. He was able to gather it all from the rubble, a shipment of a downtown section of San Francisco. He hid it in his best cave at the time, sorting and reading only during the night, his only company the quarry dogs. It taught him how to read anew. It made him want to—to have to—read again every book he had ever read before. He became afraid for it. He did not want the responsibility of having it.

He hired a coyote to deliver it to Equisa's mentor, Murrieta Tolan. The same coyote returned a month later and gave him a note from professor Tolan that said she would send it to a safe house. Her note told him to forget about *The Last Cronopio*.

He takes hold of Equisa's arm. That book, he tells her. I think it was the last thing ever printed on paper. It showed me how the world would end.

She shushes him and says that people like them, ones who can still read from paper, mustn't let on what they know about life.

I know, he says, but I'm only talking to you.

They stand at the edge of the wedding dancers. Spaces form between the swirls of couples, indicating that things are starting to end, disintegration has set in, guests are getting too drunk or tired, the bride and groom are long gone. But Equisa remains curious, raising her flattened palm to his, cousin to cousin. She thinks of the caves, him reading in them during breaks, and more and more at night, too, when he sneaks back into the quarry.

I may need a place to hide, she tells him and he nods. Are your caves cool and quiet enough?

Even the dogs would agree, he answers.

Do I need to bring my own light?

Most necessities are there in the rubble. It's a world of plenty if your needs are quiet.

After he says that, she slips him *Rayuela* which she has broken into pamphlets and tucked into various pockets of her tuxedo. Guard it with your life, she tells him. Be ready for my return. She hurries away, vanishing among the décor and capulets.

Equisa visits her cousin after he reads *Rayuela* and sends her a message telling her it is the perfect book for his series of caves. He reads it first in the order it is presented, then in the way Cortázar suggests in the epilogue, then in random. When he tells her this, that the book is a different book each time it is read in a different order of chapters and caves, Equisa travels up from her studies at UNAM and has to come see.

She falls quickly for some of the dogs who come to lay at their feet. There is something about the act of reading—their postures perhaps—and the cool of the caves that soothes the beasts. But he warns her about getting attached to any one of them. Their life expectancy in the quarry is brief, even shorter than the life expectancy of a hopper.

She learns more about his life. He is chatty, different from her, filled with words that need to spill. He doesn't have to conjure anything. She learns.

Manning the hopper in the Tijuana quarry doesn't destroy his hearing, rather it forces him to have to focus, to aim and concentrate his aural field. His auditory nerves lose their ability to process and divide general sound. They lose this ability because they lose their numbers, compliments of the hopper's thunder and the concrete it renders into re-usable powders.

This happens to almost all hoppers, at least those who live long enough to experience the erosion. The rare skill among hoppers has less to do with dexterity, strength, and knowledge than it has to do with learning how to live within brief sensory spans, those sensory spans—along with nostalgia—composing what we generally understand as life. This is why reading serves him so well. This is why he reads so much in the caves formed in the quarry by the inadvertent lay of the slabs, slabs waiting to be hoisted and crushed. Reading, more than any other solitary activity, most effectively demands focus and nostalgia.

The Tijuana quarry resides where the Agua Caliente Racetrack is built in 1929 by a Los Angeles club owner, designed by architect Wayne McAllister who is renowned for places of leisure and accessible extravagance. The racetrack survives President Cardenas' 1935 Marxist desires to refashion it into a public sports center, is rebuilt after a 1971 fire set by either a zealot or a gambler but is killed by—of all things—money, the billions that it is forced to launder during the drug boom of the early twenty-first century. You can only run so many horses, so many dogs, so many books. The quarry rises from what originally gives Agua Caliente its name, the hot springs pumping up geothermic energy, the endless supply of free power to run the hoppers, cranes, conveyors, scoops, lights, and everything else.

The quarry begins as a demolition site, first rendering the racetrack into re-usable materials, then taking on more demolition shipped from other sites in Baja and California. Entire cities are sucked through its hoppers, coming out as powder, steel, gravel, silicon, pulp, plastic block, and precious metals.

Silence is revered in the quarry. The hoppers have three breaks during which all machinery is shut down: the 10:30 coffee, the lunch, and the three o'clock refreshment. During these breaks he visits his caves and reads. Some caves are more permanent than others. Those snuggled in the rubble canyons far from the reach of the cranes tend to last longest, though hoppers never know when a certain section of the quarry might be deemed most valuable, when and where the scoops will roll in and begin mining things. The only articles he ever leaves in a cave are canteens of water and makeshift scrap-metal dishes for feeding the quarry dogs that come to sit at his feet while he reads. In his satchel he carries his tea kit, lantern, books, quires, pages, and paper scraps.

He warns Equisa again about getting too attached to the dogs. They don't know, he tells her, to stay out of caves too close to the rumble of the cranes, and they think nothing of trotting past a hopper operating at full steam.

And they are too trusting of us. They believe we are infallible with these machines.

When she returns the second time, she is on the run. She doesn't tell her cousin this and tries not to let it show. She brings *El llano en llamas*, all broken into quires so they can pass bits of it or whole stories of it back and forth. She has it this way so she can pass the Rulfo and divide it among her friends and colleagues at UNAM. It's the opposite of hoarding, she tells her cousin. Hoarding will begin the end of reading, the kind of reading we do, from paper.

Equisa suspects her cousin knows about the work of her and her mentor, but tells him anyway, an attempt at exchange on her part, her efforts to repay his openness. We aren't the usual archivists, she tells him. She studies in a program founded on the most radical ideas of Murrieta Tolan, on her principles of erasure. In fact, they keep Tolan there at UNAM, give her a lab and seclusion at the base of the volcano. Tolan argues that all writing is the erasure of knowledge, that as a species evolution earns us a single bank of finite knowledge. The earliest known petroglyph erases the first bit. What we see when we read that petroglyph, whenever we read that glyph, is the erasure dust and smudge of the knowledge it sought to represent. Ink is the exact opposite of what we believe it to be. It is obfuscation.

Tolan never claims originality in her principles of erasure. Several poetic movements in the late twentieth century operate on the notion and produce entire novels and books of verse composed solely by erasure. No one pays much attention. Prominent feminists in the early twenty-first century make compelling arguments that entire genders result from erasure.

Tolan's principles of erasure argue that all written language operates on a delicate paradox. It must erase to exist, so its existence produces extinction.

Good writing, Tolan argues, erases knowledge, but then stands as new knowledge, artificial perhaps but still a proper explication or demonstration of enlightenment. So, in the case of good writing, not much damage is done; the erosion is minimal or even reparative. But hardly any writing is good, worthwhile and timeless enough to stand in for the innate collective knowing of our species.

In Tolan's theory of erasure, metaphor's impact is twofold. That which it uses to try to illuminate and that which it attempts to illuminate are simultaneously erased. Even a well-imagined, well-wrought metaphor nonetheless eliminates lasting meaning because no metaphor can be precise, be exactly right. That is often the illusion we experience as we read an impressive metaphor—that this wholly unanticipated image *exactly* describes this complex thing, person, or sensation. We enjoy the feeling, the breadth it lends to our thinking, the breadth we think it lends to words. In the late twentieth century and early twenty-first, while Tolan is beginning her formulation, American writers and publishers accelerate the frequency and range of metaphor, value it above all other rhetorical devices, showcase it in the lyricism of the day. Award it.

The most difficult part of the Tolanist paradox to understand is the notion that we can never sense the erasure because we are in the erasure. We always think everything is fine, everything that is there before is there still. Or, another way, what we know is an accumulation of everything that has come before; but actually, as we write, as we erase, what we know is a dissimulation of everything that has come before.

She tells her cousin these things because she wants him to know what she is, what she carries inside. That she is not just some thief, some grave robber running around the desert, paying smugglers, dodging those who hunt and chase them. She is in it for purpose, not thrill.

They sit at the back of a cave, quires in their laps. Each has drawn a dog, and her mutt dozes with its head across her boots. The sound of an engine prompts both dogs to raise an ear. Her cousin, too, cocks his head at the sound.

What? she asks. They all look toward the cave entrance, a triangle of afternoon light shaped by two slabs fallen into one another.

That engine, he replies. It's different. Not from this quarry.

Taking care not to hurt the dog at her feet, she rises and then hurries to the entrance where she remains pressed to the wall, folded into a web of twisted rebar. A Jeep towing a storage trailer is parked across the flat, kinked at its hitch, forming a sort of flanked position. A woman wearing a hood and sunglasses and a man in a helmet stand behind the Jeep, their black windbreakers flickering in the breeze. They scan the cave entrance.

Equisa returns to her cousin at the back of the cave, carefully slides along the dark wall.

I can place the books outside the entrance, she says. They might just take them and go on their way. They might want me. They will certainly leave you alone.

Or? he asks.

For maybe the first time she reads him as a body. He is big, narrow-waisted. He stands with his boots pointed inward.

Or we toss food out the front and take them as they watch the dogs. We come in from the right. They will be scanning left, the dogs. How quick are you?

I'm a hopper, he replies.

I'm no good at this, she says. You will have to take yours, and then take mine, too.

He puts on his work gloves. They have wrist-guards and remind her of something from Sir Walter Scott. He hands her a length of rebar and hefts one for himself.

This will be easier than work, he assures her.

Using a strip of pliable metal and cup, she fashions a catapult for the food. Her cousin holds the mutts by their scruffs as they nip at the meat scraps. Once she releases the catapult, she knows it begins and there will be no other choice. She releases it.

These things always happen fast, but she always sees them slowly. The dogs surprise her, doing more than their part. They lope toward the food in two great strides, then curl themselves into formation and snarl at the intruders. They strike fear into them, an added bonus for Equisa and her cousin as they rush toward their targets.

She gets to the woman before she can fully turn away from the dogs. Equisa raises her bar. She hears two sounds. The first is a dark whoosh. The helmet that flies free sails silently through the air. The second is a gasp, the woman's lungs or windbreaker collapsing. The sunglasses make no sound as they fall to the sand.

Equisa looks at the rebar in her hand, still raised to the sky.

We only have a minute, her cousin says as he eases her hand down and pulls free the bar.

She gazes at her empty hands. I didn't do anything.

You are quick, he tells her. You could be a hopper.

The dogs finish their scraps and leave. The cousins gather their manuscripts and move to another cave. We should be safe, he tells Equisa. The quarry bosses won't let them poke around.

He looks at the books each has instinctively chosen, she Cortázar, he Rulfo.

Ha! he says.

Bakersfield elects to dismantle its unoccupied center and the Caliente yard begins to receive trainloads of that city's downtown. This makes the quarry landscape especially dynamic for a few days, the days when Equisa comes for more visits, the days she is ordered by Tolan to lay low after those close calls in the Baja desert. All the caves closest to the hoppers collapse and some of the more distant ones also vanish in the rumble of the scoops making room for so much new material. New caves fold and crease into existence as the Bakersfield rubble is delivered and pushed around.

During noon hour, the cousins scout and explore a few of these first, Equisa noting which form the best benches and tables. Then her cousin takes her through the more distant canyons, where he knows it will be safe for a while, where he knows they'd have at least a day's warning before any rumbling could get close enough. A trio of dogs follows them, eyeing their lunch basket.

By the time her cousin gets them to the desired cave, his hour is almost up and so he skips eating and just reads. He divides his lunch among the three dogs waiting in the shade of the cave entrance. Equisa munches a sandwich and an orange while reading some quires she has brought for herself. Midway her cousin trades his quire from *Rayuela* for her quire which he eventually figures to be Woolf's *A Room of One's Own*.

The quarry boss buzzes the hoppers' cells and her cousin has to return to work. He suggests that Equisa go back to her hotel but she stays and reads in the cave until three o'clock refreshment, when he returns. She greets him with a wave and a grin and tells him she explores the quarry a little, taking walking breaks, always going toward the safe direction he showed her.

I came upon a crumpled library, she tells him as he finds a slab to sit on, in the coolest recess of the lean-to. Segments of its pillars, she says, and its lintel stone carved in Latin. But no pages. Not a scrap.

They're looted before demolition, he says. Library rubble is the worst place to look for books. Try sports arenas, next time, stadiums. He sits up straight, correcting his posture, trying to stretch away the pain of work. She sits easily among the slabs of concrete, legs crossed, one arm resting on the end of a propped slab, the other across her lap, thumbed to a pamphlet of *Rayuela*. Equisa's dressed as an explorer, a colonialist, with several pockets.

Her cousin looks past her for a moment, out the cave entrance. The dogs are gone. Everybody seems gone. The quarry is silent, its rubbled hills white. She can tell her cousin tries to focus his hearing on her, before looking at her. She knows he is concentrating his aural nerves after working the hopper, to hear before seeing. She helps him by rustling the pages in her lap.

Why do you do this with your books? he asks her. Take them apart and pass them around? Isn't that dangerous? Won't you lose them?

It's my meager attempt to save them, she answers. Actually. She carefully divides the *Rayuela* pamphlet into pages, meticulously tearing each one along the straight edge of the fold.

He winces, stretching his spine. This far back in the cave they have to set up a lantern to prepare tea and read. He kneels and does this, first finding a cranny in which to wedge the lantern. He fires the little camp burner and balances the water pot and as they wait for it to come to a boil she explains what she's doing.

I see you wince, pretending it's from the pain of work, she says. But it's from me tearing the pages. But really, I am trying to save them. The hoarding's begun, going faster than we anticipated. She throws metaphors at him, knowing he'll wince even more. She smiles.

A treasure hoard is the easiest to plunder, she says. Hoarded food rots much faster, is easiest to poison. Anything hoarded by the few is envied by the masses, then vilified. It's the theory of Alexandria, she explains. They tried to save all books by collecting them. But in reality, doomed them.

Except those that got out. Those volumes and pages and scraps that got out. Half-burnt pages that floated along with the ashes.

But she sees that he has lost focus with his screwed-up hearing, that he probably can't even say who speaks these last words. She or he or the gray dog that has wandered to the entrance of their cave and is staring at them.

Looking at the hound, Equisa quotes from the page her cousin is holding, the Woolf for which he's traded: as if it too questioned the universe, something seemed lacking, something seemed different.

Twenty-one

FLACO DROVE ME TO the Tijuana holding bins. His jeep was all open and the highway speed drowned our voices. He put on some music but all we could hear of it between the engine roar and the turbulence was the bass. I managed to leave work a little early, but we were still racing sunset. Flaco wrapped his orange dreadlocks in a bandana and gave himself to the wind. On the straight-aways, he gazed at the ocean, one wrist slack over the wheel.

Our boards were tied overhead, just in case. Sometimes, when the predominant surf was blown out or flat, little unnamed coves would present themselves with glassy, perfectly shouldered three-footers. You could spot them from the highway if you knew how to use the sun's low slant.

In my fist, I clutched a piece of paper with the call numbers of three books that had been sent to storage. I chose them according to different patterns of obscurity—temporal, thematic, and cultural. The first was a book on volcanoes from 1954. The second was a 1965 argument against the validity of the double-helix. The third was a 2003 geography text. Flaco seemed amused by how I subjected the paper to the wind.

Near the southern edge of Tijuana, we veered inland. Boards overhead, we might have looked like lost surfers among the compressed and ramshackle *colonias*, but Flaco navigated the pitted streets without hesitation. The jeep, black and sand-scuffed, big tires, high clearance, appeared born out of any of the tin-roofed auto shops that marked every corner.

Flaco paused to let a vendor push his cart across the street, throttled the jeep. The *vendedor* advertised tacos stuffed with head meats.

Flaco leaned toward me, grinning. "Hongry?"

He yanked us onward, into the hills and mesas covered in a mix of formal and informal housing, *colonias* designated by tire stairways. When I tried to figure our direction, I realized Flaco's immediate goal was to find high ground. None of the streets or oil roads or alleys were named. Given the fleeting nature of all the buildings, landmarks were hard to come by. There was no sense of the nearby ocean.

Taking a path that wound along the alluvial spill of a waste heap, Flaco brought us to an overlook. Hills, white with shacks and laundry and faded cars, rolled up from the burning yellow line of the ocean. But Flaco was looking the other way, east, searching an even more vast expanse of jammed hillsides. To the north, I could see the sphere marking the downtown cultural center, so far away it looked like a soccer ball.

The air at the base of the alluvial fan had been dank with sewage and rot, nearly unbreathable. Up here, it had an almost pleasant tang, like paint thinner.

I was still clutching the paper with the call numbers. Flaco spotted some kind of landmark. He sucked his teeth, registered the view, eyed me as though I were about to steal his wave. I tucked the slip of paper into the back pocket of my jeans.

Catalina, Cisco, and I knew the holding bins were not going to match the ones shown on the company's website. We knew, when we shipped our dormant holdings, what it would mean to send them to Tijuana. But we were given a sudden deadline and an impossible budget. None of us had gone to visit the holdings. It felt like sending a very old and very senile aunt, someone vaguely met once at a wedding, to a nursing home.

We face arguments for keeping books like these, severely outdated and inaccurate studies on volcanoes, genetics, and geography. Historians claim they might need them to chart the trajectory of knowledge. Scholars seek the irony, the intellectual high ground and amusement found in unenlightened past cultures, sometimes bits of forethought embedded in quaint style and content. Scientists maintain their need for recording error. Sentimentalists see nothing beyond the physical wonder of a bound volume, nostalgia rendered solid and contained.

I studied Flaco as he drove us toward whatever landmark he had spotted. The street was pitted and a lot of the informal vendors had pitched their stands beyond the gutters, ready for evening traffic. So Flaco had to concentrate, stiff-arm the wheel. He was a reader. I really only knew him as that and a surfer. He must have been curious about these dormant volumes, about the general fate of books in this world. Maybe his life terrarium could only feel complete if he decorated it with a little shelf of untouched volumes or accented a far corner with a brightly painted shipping bin full of unread novels.

At the Michigan conference where I got to know Catalina, where we read together in the Landmark, we were shown an intricate dollhouse filled with working miniatures. Lamps, fans, fireplaces, clocks. Its library featured leather reading chairs surrounded by book-shelved walls. Upon close inspection, we saw that the book spines bore titles. I joked that the books were real, that we could read them if we drank a potion and grew small. Our guide, using tweezers and white gloves, slipped free Hardy's *Return of the Native* and showed us that the miniatures were indeed real, complete, readable. "All of them?" I asked, fulfilling my role as fool and foil.

•

Atop a mesa, Flaco parked the jeep in a gravel cutout. The broad flat was divided by a chain link fence. On one side, was a vast wrecking yard. On the other side, were the shipping bins. Below us, on all sides, were myriad *colonias*, rolling toward the ocean, toward the eastern and southern mountains, toward the northern city. Across this sea of ramshackle housing, we could see another mesa rising up like an island, the one holding the notorious prison.

On our mesa, the random spread of the wrecking yard contrasted the neat stacks of the shipping bins. A slight curve in the fence gave the whole thing a yin-yang effect. The wrecking yard was mostly for cars, but other things had been rendered, too. Whole houses, stacks of refrigerators, washers, dryers, appliances I couldn't identify.

I pressed myself to the wrecking yard fence, liking the feel of the warm chain-link, the galvanized scent. The nearest pile was a cinder cone of cell phones, high enough to block the low sun. The breeze blew through it, made that ghost-town sound of abandonment, and brought a new smell, a fresh glue scent.

Flaco drew beside me and inhaled. "You could almost get high off it," he said. He put a hand to my shoulder to pull me back, but not in time. A yard dog, a Doberman with the stride of a thoroughbred, appeared from behind the cell phones. It remained silent during its elegant run, as though in a dream. But it hit the fence hard with its forepaws, rattling the entire front. It growled and barked, left its teeth bared as it stood on hind legs and faced us. It eyed Flaco, ignored me.

We backed away, Flaco pulling my shirt. "Nothing like a good junkyard dog to get the heart started," he said.

"Or stopped," I replied.

The Doberman stood its ground, zeroed in on Flaco, as

we shuffled toward the bin yard gate. Flaco stopped me from getting too close to that entrance.

"Unless you want to meet another one." He smiled, but it was strained as he scanned the open area beyond the closed gate. "I think the bin one has three heads or something."

He drew his cell and spoke to someone named Walter.

A man wearing a straw hat came out of the long Airstream trailer that fronted the bin yard. The trailer shone bright, reflecting the deep yellow of near-sunset. Red and white geraniums hedged the base of the trailer and the man paused to check the flowers, digging his fingers into the soil to see if they needed water.

The trailer ran horizontal to the thousands of vertically lined bins behind it. Some of the bins were stacked two-high, with narrow ladders leading up to the second-story doors. It was easy to imagine them inhabited, a city of bin dwellers, with color-coded blocks to find your way home. Red, yellow, blue, green, orange.

The man rose from his flowers, waved to us, then went around to the back of the trailer.

I looked at Flaco.

"The dog," he said. He remained still and I did the same.

•

THE MAN UNLOCKED A little side gate for us and waved us into the yard. I let Flaco go first. I moved my slip of paper with the call numbers to the front pocket of my jeans.

The man greeted us. He was Walter. He tipped his hat brim and shook my hand, then chatted with Flaco. He called Flaco Emilio, then just Lio as they spoke about a good time they had downtown with some women neither of them could name. Their Spanish was peppered with too much jargon for me to understand everything.

Their conversation ended abruptly and they looked at me. Flaco lifted his brow and nodded toward my pocket. Walter adjusted his straw hat. He wore a Mexican World Cup team soccer shirt, jeans and cowboy boots. The boots almost made him tall enough to reach Flaco's shoulders.

I handed Walter the slip of paper. The pencil lead had smeared, but the titles and numbers were still legible. Walter eyed the paper, raised a waiting hand, and disappeared behind the trailer. I checked the distance between myself and the gate, gave myself a one-step head-start.

Flaco squinted at me.

"Lio," I said. "You prefer that?"

"When we're not at Brigadoons," he replied.

"I feel pretty far from there," I said.

The fence running between the two yards was well-kept, taut from post to post. It tapered into a thin gray line before vanishing over the far end of the mesa, like a spider's thread. But there were intermittent gates, some wide enough for vehicles. Flaco—Lio—was studying the pile of cell phones on the other side.

"I didn't know you were friends with the yard boss," I said. "When I asked you to come with me."

"Walter's not the boss. That's not his office." He nodded toward the Airstream. "He runs the dogs for all of the yards."

"Trains them?" I asked. I watched for Walter's appearance from either end of the trailer.

"He brokers them, places them, makes sure they're cared for. He has access to all the yards." Flaco stretched his arms, the way he did whenever he spotted an incoming set. "Rule the dogs," he said, "rule the city."

Twenty-two

WALTER APPEARED FROM BEHIND the Airstream driving a golf cart. It was modified to hold four people and had a hitch on the back like the one we used to haul the burn bin. The slip of paper with my call numbers was pinned to the center of the steering wheel, where a scorecard would go. Flaco offered me shotgun, but I asked to ride in back. Walter took us down the center road, paved and wide enough for the delivery trucks. Far down the center, a crane loomed above the yard, the crook of its neck topped with the Mexican flag.

I looked back to find the dog. Like a farm animal, it lay in a bed of straw beneath a sunshade. Dark as the shadows, it took me a moment to discern its form. It raised its head and gave us an over-the-shoulder look as we sped away. A small mutt, ignoring everything, pillowed its head on the giant's relaxed ankles. A third dog, with a kind of mustache, sat upright and still.

Without looking back as he drove, Walter whistled twice. Mustache bolted around to the front side of the office trailer, maybe to watch our boards. The other two dogs remained as they were.

"What are their names," I asked, leaning into the wind of our ride.

"El Santo, Blue Demon, and Místico." Walter grinned over the wheel.

"Which *luchador* would you want in the ring with you?"

Walter laughed hard, got his shoulders into it. "Which one for you, Gato?"

"Místico," I answered. "His mask had no mouth. Only eyes."

Walter told us more about the dogs and how their *luchador* names fit. Místico was a good choice, the mustache one sent to guard our boards. He didn't have near the size and strength of El Santo, but his loyalty was unmatched by any dog Walter had ever known. And little Blue Demon was the terror of the group, almost always looking for a fight, even with his teammates.

"He may look small and sleepy right now," Walter told us. "But once he hears Místico from the front, he'll be the first to the fence. He'll climb halfway up the chain-link. Like Blue Demon over the ropes."

•

WALTER TURNED ONTO A crossroad, taking us into the shadows of the bins. The bins were the size and shape of freight cars and several were stacked two-high, with those spindly ladders leading up to their auxiliary doors. The auxiliaries, cut into the huge front-swing accesses, reminded me of dog doors. The bins looked in good shape, brightly painted and sturdy. I could imagine them in Flaco's terrarium, or in some kid's model train world. They had stenciled numbers on their fronts, bright silver spin vents on top.

The gridded roadways were kept neat, free of trash and weeds. Even though the sweep and rise of the neighboring rendering yard loomed ocean-like to the west, I started to feel better about the books. The waft of the junkyard was more chemical than rot. Some of the piles rose higher than the bins and their metal parts, like fake snow, reflected the falling sun.

Walter stopped to check my call numbers, then studied a text on his cell. He sent a text, then smiled at Flaco and me as he awaited the reply.

"How do those numbers work?" I asked.

He showed us, underlining each with his fingernail. His

knuckles were slender, like those of a doctor, not the black-creased hands of a mechanic. The first number was a quadrant, the second a row, the third a bin. "And the last," he said with a shrug, "its place inside."

"Its place inside?" I asked.

"He's just the dog guy," said Flaco. "He knows all the yards in TJ, and they know him. But he's expert on none. He minds his own business, which is a good way to go about the yards."

The text arrived and Walter continued the drive. He drove us into a quadrant tucked far into the southwest corner, alongside a section of the junkyard heaped with crashed cars, shattered windshields flopping outward like torn pages.

Walter parked in front of a line of four green bins. He pointed. "These have your books."

Behind the green bins, the mesa dropped into a chasm too steep to hold any shacks. There was a gate in the fence separating us from the junkyard. It was piped and formal but had no lock.

Walter sent another text and waited. I left the cart and walked between the bins, saying I needed to stretch my legs. I went to the back fence to peer down the ravine. Both sides were laced with detritus, like cobwebs or flotsam left after a flood. The bottom crease was clogged with clothes and paper. It was easy to imagine rotting books. On the far side, lower than our mesa, the rolling and endless *colonias* began again.

When I returned to the front of the bins, Walter was ready to open a door for us. He peeked at his cell for the combination, then spun the lock. He freed the big doors. They swung open with a series of groans that echoed among the bins.

After finding the books floating in the sea and seeing the papery waste of the ravine, it was better than I expected. But not anything Cisco and Catalina—or any librarian—would want to see. The books were still packed in their cardboard cartons. The cartons were lined two-deep on shelves running the length of the bin. The shelves were three-high along each wall of the bin. With a tinny chime overhead, the spin vent let in air and dappled light.

Like this, the books would last as long as they would in a normal household. It would be very hard to access any of the cartons on the top shelf and any of the ones in the back. Each box had a stenciled number. And that was it. The last number on the call sheet brought you to a box of one hundred, just like our assessment cartons.

Flaco and Walter used their phone lights to search for the number of my first book, the one on volcanoes. I poked at the cartons in front.

The life-span of a library book is about fifty checkouts. Librarians try to argue for twenty-five, but that's a funding issue. The life-span of a typical cloth-bound volume sitting unread is impossible to gauge because there are too many production and environmental variables. I figured that in this setting, any decently cloth-bound book would last about a hundred years, starting from new. My volcano book had about forty left, depending on how often it was checked out before it was sent here.

Ancient books—rare books—last so long because they were made with a lot more care and they were lucky. They either tumbled into a dry and antiseptic nook, or they fell into the kid-gloved hands of a bibliophile.

I looked at the shelves as Flaco and Walter searched the bin. Was this a better fate than Cuervo? I would get a different answer from J.B. D'Acquisto than I would from any of his readers. I found myself wondering what Valeria would say.

And what would Equisa say?

Flaco found the carton. It was on the second shelf toward the back. It was behind the front line of boxes, pressed to the wall, so he had to pull one carton out to gain access. Walter had to help him ease the cartons to the floor.

Flaco waved his hand over the sealed box. "Your honors, Jack."

For some reason, some sensation, I looked behind me. It was not a look of paranoia or permission. It was more wishful than that, more fanciful. Looking for Marisa or Cisco. Catalina or Valeria. A dog. A *luchador*. Beyond the open swing of the doors was nothing but the expanse of the bin yard. One of the doors, suspended by the ocean breeze, shielded my view of the rendering yard, so there were only the bins, neatly lined, occasionally stacked, colors amplified in low sun—and the distant crane above like a robotic arm. If Flaco's life view was accurate, then this was me at the moment, a librarian in a world of suspension patrolled by loyal dogs.

Walter loaned me his pen-knife and I cut the seal to the carton. Flaco and I dug through the books, searching for the 1954 volume on volcanoes. The collection appeared random. The Dewey Decimal numbers on the spines were meaningless in this container. Flaco would occasionally show me a find—a slender thing about tree house living in 1968, a biography of an entomologist who saved the dragonflies of Singapore, a how-to book about building your own aquatic vehicles.

I spotted the book on volcanoes and freed it from the pack. Not really knowing what to do, I showed it to Walter and Flaco. Both nodded and smiled. They watched as I re-sorted the volumes we had removed. I placed the volcano book on top, last. We gazed at the books. This would be the last time they would be seen. In this life, this expanding and contracting life of ours, now defined by this bin yard, I could tell. I could know.

•

WALTER TOOK US TO another bin, another of the green ones, two removed from the first. Again, he texted for the combination. A dog barked as we waited. When I looked anxiously at Walter he shook his head.

"That's King," he told us, "from next door."

He opened the bin doors. The view was the same. The book cartons were stacked two-deep, three shelves high. Flaco found the box number quickly, in front on the second shelf. When he reached to scoot it down, I tapped his shoulder and told him not to bother, that it was enough to know we could get this far. He gave us a sad look. I thought briefly of indulging him, letting this reader dig for the most outdated of volumes, a thing arguing against the existence of the double-helix.

I told him we could dig for the third, the 2003 geography book. And that we should hurry so that we could drive back to Ensenada alongside the sunset, maybe get to Calafia while the whales were still visible.

Walter led us to the final green bin, the one next to the rendering yard fence. King, far off amid the piles, barked again and a cloud of starlings rose into the sky. As they swam in murmuration, undulating into Möbius strips against the blue, I imagined them as a junk pile lifted and stirred by the wind, a flock of discarded cell phones or broken spectacles.

But the combination Walter received for the final bin did not work. He tried three times, then shrugged. He texted again. We watched the starlings. When the reply came, Walter told us we had to go, that he had to get to another yard to take care of the dogs. He turned to lead us back to the cart.

Flaco raised a hand to stop him. "Walter," he said.

"I don't think your boxes will be in there."

Flaco went to the auxiliary door. He was a head taller than this cut-out entrance. He fingered the padlock, the kind opened with a bottom key. From his jeans pocket he removed what first looked like a wallet. But it contained a shiny set of picks. He sought Walter's permission before proceeding.

"But we don't go in," said Walter. "Only see."

Flaco popped the lock in less than a minute. It made the sound of a coin dropped into a meter. Flaco stood back and let Walter open the little door for us. Flaco shone his phone light and we peered inside. The bin had the same shelves as the others, but the shelves held barrels, hundreds of them, neatly lined, with iridescent numbers.

I thought of the preserved hare I saw the first time I met Marisa, in the Pátzcuaro library, the way it appeared to be sleeping in its fluid, waiting to be freed, to leap along the slopes of the volcano. But these barrels were bigger and made of metal, not glass.

Flaco closed the door and reset the lock.

We were thinking the same thing, and knew that, so we didn't speak it. The books in the ocean were once briefly in that bin—if they ever got there in the first place. If their first destination wasn't a seaside cliff. Neither of us wanted to imagine what was in the barrels. We wanted to get away from them as fast as possible.

Walter drove us back to the jeep. The slip of paper with my call numbers, still pinned to the steering wheel's hub, flapped in the wind of our ride. The starlings continued to swim above us, the entire flock twisting then hanging, twisting then hanging.

Twenty-three

Flaco spun us south down the Baja highway. Over my right shoulder, the sun touched the horizon, spilling its light over the sea. The breeze curled hard around the jeep's windshield, muting us back into our own thoughts. At times, we pointed at things that amused or amazed us. An old-style Westfalia, aqua blue and cream, parked atop the cliffs. A frigate bird wobbling overhead like a model plane. A hot-air balloon appearing lost over the mountains.

But I could see that Flaco was thinking of the yards we had just visited. My expression probably mirrored his, furrowed against the wind. We would dream about the starlings, the dogs, their *luchador* namesakes, the bins, the shelved boxes. We would dream about the barrels. And that was where our dreams would part, mine the soft nightmares of a librarian, his those of someone who could pick the locks of the bin yards, who could gain access because he knew the keeper of the dogs.

About the lost books, he was probably sadder than I. He was a reader and had to always know there was another good book waiting, another find. Before I became a librarian, my dreams would often inhabit the books I was reading. It still happened, as it did during my last beach nap, but rarely.

•

We reached our table at Calafia too late for whale spotting, but the sky offered plenty for our thoughts. Thin clouds feathered the horizon, their bottoms yellow over a gray sea. A single strand of orange roped toward the evening star.

Four levels down the cliffs, we chose a landing whose other

tables were unoccupied. Our waitress brought us margaritas cloudy with fresh lime and a bowl of clams steamed in garlic and wine. In front of me, she set down a small plate of coarse salt and I knew that Marisa had seen me. Maybe she had spotted me hopping from the jeep, maybe at the bar placing our order to save the waitress an extra trip along the escarpment.

Flaco looked comfortable, in his element, elegant in the way he eased back and crossed his legs, let the food and drink catch the twilight and torch flames.

"Where does Walter keep his dogs?" I asked.

"He has a ranch in the valley," Flaco answered. He told me how Walter found them in the streets, abandoned fence dogs tossed aside by yard owners. Sometimes Flaco would hunt the Tijuana neighborhoods with him, looking for certain breeds and mixes, spotting particular behaviors, dogs who would sit sentry-like at corners, others who would stand guard while the rest of the pack gnawed discarded bones.

"The official population of TJ is 1.8 million," he said. "The most accurate studies indicate something over five million. That makes for a lot of dogs. Probably a million."

"How many does Walter keep?"

"I think he has around three hundred spread over all the yards and ranches. He never keeps more than twenty at a time at his ranch."

"Do you have one?"

Flaco finally reached for his drink. "I go and visit Walter's."

He took a hardy pull of the margarita, squinted against the tang of lime and tequila. "Oh, that's good. Good as I heard." He placed three clams onto his plate, sprinkled them with a pinch of the coarse salt.

"At the top," he said. "Where we came in. There was a

woman watching from way down behind the bar. Very nice, in a white dress. I was hoping she would look at me—but she was looking at you."

"My ex," I said, though I thought about letting him think I had somehow outshined him. "She and her husband own this place. He cooks, she plans."

"You're sleeping with her."

"Only when he's out of town."

"When does he return?"

I sipped my drink. "Do you have an ex?"

"I have two. But they've moved on."

The orange trace in the sky had reddened. Another star appeared by the first. From somewhere on the rocks below us, sea lions barked back and forth. Flaco watched the sea.

"I'm sorry about your books, Jack."

"I expected worse." I ate one clam. It tasted like the ocean and I began to feel hungry. The margarita was strong, very tart, with big heavy ice cubes that didn't float.

Marisa and three waitresses appeared on our landing. As they descended from the steps, each woman smiled at us, one by one, Marisa last. The waitresses wore sleeveless dresses with colors and patterns that reminded me of the Westfalia we saw parked along the highway.

The women gathered beneath a torch and Marisa proceeded to point out places on the landings below, all the while giving quiet instructions. Flaco and I tried to be discreet with our glances, but it was a difficult thing to avoid with the sky and sea as background.

I wasn't sure if Marisa would come by for an introduction. This was the perfect place for her, and Jimbo was the one who had brought her to it. A bar or restaurant, even a hotel or resort, wouldn't have been challenge enough for her. Calafia was unique, hacked as it was into these black rugged cliffs, poised above the gray whales' Pacific migration. Despite its natural setting and good location, it had failed in all of its previous incarnations—exclusive club, party bar, special event venue. Most believed it was fated to the Baja curse which plagued a lot of coastal ventures, an unknown force that steered away tourists and locals, rendered the grandest designs into instant ghost towns and ruins. Marisa, uninterested in Baja legends and curses, was the one who had adjusted its shape and light and accesses into an inviting and irresistible stop.

When she was done with her instructions and had answered the waitresses' questions, Marisa sent them away. Two descended and one went up. Marisa approached our table, backlit by the torch, the breeze pushing her white dress about her.

Flaco stood to shake her hand and I clumsily followed. She gave me an amused look and then reached for Flaco's handshake, locking eyes and smiling. I introduced them. I called him Emilio Mendes-Kohl, then Lio.

"You're not a librarian," she said.

I told her how Flaco had helped me track down the dormant books in Tijuana. When she raised her brow for more explanation, he told her how enchanting this place was. She made us sit back down and told us she would send us another round and that we better not try to pay for anything.

Flaco watched her ascend the stone staircase. I felt good about fulfilling my deal with him, grateful toward Marisa for helping me honor it, recognizing it, raising it.

He sipped his drink. "I think you have at least one more night," he said.

"He returns tomorrow or the next day," I said. "We don't know yet."

“There’s a swell leaving Hawaii today,” Flaco replied. “It should get here by tomorrow evening. Some of the pros there are chasing it.”

I pictured surfers at an airport in Honolulu, checking their best boards through security. I pictured them on the plane, looking down at the ocean, racing the eastward swell. And then I thought of Equisa, the torn corner of paper tucked into the coin pocket of her jeans, making her way across the Mexican desert.

Twenty-four

I HELPED MARISA CLOSE. I collected the empties from all seven landings and put them in recycling bins. At the top, I returned all the liquor bottles to their correct section in front of the mirror and then wiped down the bar. Marisa flipped chairs while the one remaining waitress swept the tile floor with a push broom. When we were done, the waitress left. Marisa and I performed what was always the last chore, the dowsing of the torches, from bottom to top.

We descended the night steps lit by candles in the cliff wall. I held the rail. She held my hand.

"You've made a friend," she said. "That's good."

"He's a Brigadoon. We've surfed together for ten years."

"Still. He wants more from you."

"He also checks books from the library."

"What does he do?"

"He can pick a lock and navigate the yards. Those people seem to know him." We reached the first landing and paused to listen to the sea lions, still restless and barking in the night. "I'm not going to ask Flaco more than that."

"You said his name was Lio."

"Flaco's his Brigadoon name. Probably what they call him, too, when he goes up to surf the California beaches."

"He looks more strong than skinny. More *fuerto* than *flaco*."

"He looks skinny on his board," I explained. "Because he's tall for a surfer. He looks like splinters of iron, in his wetsuit, crouched into a wave. Besides, surfers only accept names that undermine. Like Flea or Toad."

"You know what you look like, Jack? Crouched in a wave?"

"A bad surfer, fearing for his life."

She smiled and led us to the next staircase. "More eager than that. Trying to figure things out."

As we descended toward the second landing, I told her about finding the books, about how it was in the yard and the bins. I told her about the last bin full of barrels and how all those books were missing.

"Will you tell Cat?"

"Yes," I said. "But not Cisco."

"You think all those lost books will crush him?"

"Not the lost ones," I explained. "The ones in the boxes. With Deweys that don't really matter."

"It's still how you find them," she argued. "It's still how you start."

•

ON THE BOTTOM LANDING—the seventh—the surf spray had already gotten heavy. One of the torches had been dowsed by the geyser of a big wave. The sea lions were loud. I peered over the edge to try to make out their forms on the rocks below, but it was much too dark. All I could really see was the sea foam, white stirred into black water, laced over black rocks.

Marisa capped the remaining torch and we hurried to the steps to escape the spray of the next wave. On our way up, we pinched the candles embedded in the cliffs. I was able to reach the higher ones. When alone, she usually carried a brass snuffer for this task.

"Thanks for letting me come along for this," I said as we climbed. "I know you enjoy this part alone. The solitude of it. So thanks."

I could tell Jimbo had decided to return tomorrow, early. She released my hand somewhere along the last ascension. She bowed her head and stretched her arms and shoulders.

"Next time you go to the yards," she said. "Take me, too."

I feared that every time like this with her would be the last. That I would later get a text at the library: No more. Or something brief and final like that. Though that would be her trying to be like me. The first real librarians, those medieval monks, had to snuff hundreds of candles as they made their final night passes through the labyrinthine shelves and underground caverns. One missed flame could mean the end of the entire collection. The light that allowed them access also threatened everything they knew.

The snuffer Marisa used was one I had purchased for her during one of my trips to the Edinburgh public library. It was a nice brass replica of a fourteenth-century piece. I gave it to her on the fifth anniversary of our divorce, told her I thought of her when I saw it, pictured her dowsing the candles of Calafia.

•

SHE CLOSED THE DOORS to the bar and we said good night. I kissed her on the cheek. Only then did we realize she was my only ride home. Flaco and his jeep were long gone.

"I can get a cab back to the EPL," I said. "My car's there."

"Don't be a martyr, Jack."

She drove the night highway like a Baja pro. I would watch the moon and stars over the dark sea, then turn to study her profile, her hands light on the wheel, her bare arms illuminated by the dashboard. Her car was nice, quiet and smooth after Flaco's jeep. Everything in her life was nicer now.

She told me I should talk to Cat about the bins and that I should also talk to her more about what she was doing with the books.

"You two," she said. "You're not *always* on the same page."

Twenty-five

Even though Marisa told me not to, I decided to spend the night in the library again. I used *Equisa* to read myself to sleep, told myself I would put it in the burn bin after, toss it into Cuervo along with the others. After showing more of Equisa's past, her adventures with her cousin, her returns to Murrieta Tolan's lab at the base of Popocatepetl, the story returned to the present moment, picking up where it had left her alone in the Chihuahuan desert, kneeling beside the coyote's grave, wearing borrowed clothes, in pursuit of the torn corner of paper, the *ure*. She keeps traveling, getting to the shore of the Sea of Cortez, aiming north across the water to Baja. As I read, I felt her coming up behind me, the figure that vanishes as soon as you look over your shoulder. Eight more pages, sixteen minutes.

> Equisa kneels in the sand by the coyote's tomb and craves what she fears. It's those last three letters she saw, ink on paper: *ure*. That fragment of a word on top of a torn wedge of words, a fragment in a fragment. She craves any words on paper, the worst thing, a fearful commodity. But any words on paper will help her read the rest of the torn wedge, the rest of the page, the rest of the book.
>
> The woman in the DEA windbreaker who takes Equisa's hair and clothes has the scrap. Has she found it yet, tucked in the tiny coin pocket of Equisa's jeans? What will she do with it? Confiscate it? Burn it? *Read* it? Read secretly then burn it?
>
> Equisa notices the first brittle spikes of dawn on the

desert horizon. They make her thirsty, make her think of ice, make her think she'd best start moving before she dies in the sand with this coyote. She rubs the chopped remains of her hair, imagines she is washing it in the moonlight. One final time she looks at the tomb she fashioned for the coyote, sees the name she pounded out for him on the tin jackal head. The last book you read, she says to him, was Rulfo's *El Llano en Llamas*. You'll do okay.

Before sunrise she makes it to the outskirts of the vast spread of buildings that has no name, that never becomes a city. She is from a city that no longer exists, that has long passed through the renderings of quarries, that vanishes center outward. But what's it like to be born in a place like this, to be from a place such as this, a place you can't really name? A place that never *is*? You say Chihuahua, but that doesn't tell much of anything. You say southern Chihuahua and that at least separates you from the ugliness of the north. That place, you say. It's a big place, you know?

She hopes to catch the dawn bus full of workers and ride out of Chihuahua as soon as possible. This state has never brought her anything but misery and despair—almost death, if it weren't for that coyote and her own ability to read and conjure him. She misses her cousin.

At the corner bus stop, standing with others in dawn light, for the first time she is conscious of her borrowed clothes, the milky jeans, the Team Mexico soccer jersey, and the tennis shoes. Shorn and dressed like this, she stands toward the rear of the gathering.

All the other women, men, boys, and girls carry lunch pails or baskets. They each stare at her in twenty second increments, register her in clichés: discarded mistress, whore, addict, heading home while we go to work. Maybe one or two of them identify her true addiction. She endures this in the bus wait, knowing they'll be finished with her soon. What possible impression could interest any of them at this hour of day?

I'm an archivist, she tells them. I got sidetracked in the desert.

She is thinking too much because she has nothing to read from paper, no ink to caress with her eyes. Anything will do. She even yearns for the scrap of cereal box—paint on cardboard—the woman in the DEA windbreaker burned. Anything that is remotely akin to ink on paper would at least guide her nerves, keep them from spraying outward in all directions. The others in the bus gathering watch their tiny screens, brush their fingers and eyes there, tap their ears on occasion.

She closes her eyes covers her ears and recalls the last real ink: *ure*. She goes down the chute of the first letter, up and over the second, enjoys the interrupted circle of the last, the diametrical return.

She rides a morning bus all the way to Navajoa, mainly to get out of Chihuahua as quickly as possible. Navajoa is a place of six bus stations and one train depot all clinging together. At one time it is a city, a little one, yet a city. But not much remains except these stations and the vendors inside them, the food kiosks and laundromats. From there she catches the coast train north and strains her neck to get glimpses of the Sea of Cortez. She buys dried figs, another cactus pear soda, and crumbly cheese from an aisle vendor. The vendor, only a girl, hands Equisa her phone for payment, stares at her forlornly as Equisa brushes the screen with the tip of her ring finger.

Gum? asks the girl. For after?

No thank you, says Equisa. But then she realizes that the girl has been staring at her for more than twenty seconds, maybe twice that long.

Equisa stares back. You read? she whispers to the girl. The girl just tilts her head but maintains eye contact.

You *have* something?

Gum, she answers.

Let me see first.

The girl holds up a stick of gum crooked in her palm so only Equisa can see it. It has a wrapper. The wrapper looks like paper and has words on it. The girl curls her fingers over the words expertly, before Equisa can read.

How much? How much for the gum?

The girl brushes in the amount and hands Equisa the cell so she can see the amount on the screen. The gum will cost more than her train and bus tickets and food combined. Equisa forwards the payment and the girl passes the gum to her, palm to palm, the warm paw of a dog.

The girl hurries away, up the aisle, into the forward cars. Equisa knows she will have to wait until she disembarks from the train, but just the promise of the paper and ink she tucks into the coin pocket of her jeans soothes her nerves a bit. She will not make the same mistake she did with the coyote on the bus through Chihuahua, a mistake that got him killed, almost her, too. She will resist even a glance at the letters until she is long gone from this train. Until she is utterly alone.

But through the ozone of the train motor she can smell the gum. From the mere tips of the letters the vendor lets her see, Equisa knows the gum is from a confectioner in Uruguay—Uruguay, the last country to print on paper. The fragrance is licorice. They flavor the gum with star anise. She closes her eyes, cups her ears and imagines she is reading by scent, the way blind people once read by touch. Uruguay is green and level, not at all similar to the dry and sparse desert slopes and crags of Sonora. But Sonora has the sea, and Uruguay has the sea, and people she meets always forget that Sonora has the sea, the Sea of Cortez, narrow as it is. She is born by the Sea of Cortez, up the shore from where this train glides, in a city that vanishes later.

Black Star. That's the name of the gum creased into the coin pocket of her borrowed jeans. She only sees the top edges and spikes of the letters when the vendor girl flashes the gum for her, but the shapes drop like window shades and she sees and reads. Black Star. It is flavored with star anise harvested from the plains west of Montevideo. They dye it black, black as ink.

She wants to chew that blackness, taste it, while she reads the words on paper. Black Star.... In a way the craving is worse with the words so close, tucked in her pocket. But she knows, recalling the coyote's name pounded into the tin jackal head, that she must wait until she disembarks in Guaymas, until the vendor girl is away northward on the train, far removed from Equisa's circle of paper and ink and death. She thinks of the letter e. And eats her dried figs and crumbly cheese. And drinks her cactus pear soda.

In Guaymas she hurries from the train station. It feels good to find her way through a city, though it is small. As she navigates the noon-hour sidewalks busy with workers taking lunch, she plans chewing the gum and reading the wrapper in a special place, a unique moment. Here and there desert hills jut from the neighborhoods of Guaymas. The hill names are passed from generation to generation by the kids who climb and play on them. The hill names are forgotten, but not by her.

Equisa ascends one of her favorites, The Witch's Hat, one she loves when she is a child, one she gets to know after her family moves here, their adopted city. She switchbacks her way up, finding the open sand between rust-color stone and cholla, keeping an eye out for rattlers cooling beneath outcrops.

At the top she takes her place on a stone worn smooth by thousands before her. She looks over the city of Guaymas, notes the tile roof of her old home, the noon sun blazing in the solar panel, blazing on a plain of brilliant points across the city. She eases her eyes over the bay and the Sea of Cortez, the soft blue, the blur above the sharp horizon. The beginning of a distant thunderstorm smudges the southern end of the sea's horizon. In a patch of sand nearby, a hare crouches in the brown sand between rocks, electing to camouflage rather than run. It folds itself up, long ears back, locust wings.

Stay there, Little One, she whispers. Stay with me as I read. Read you a story.

The hare remains crouched, still as stone, believing itself artful and undetected. Equisa savors her craving and fear a moment longer before removing the gum from her coin pocket. Immediately the licorice scent rises in the pure air. Looking away so that she doesn't see the words on the wrapper, Equisa slides the stick of gum free, opens the foil. She hides the words on paper—ink on paper!—in the curl of three fingers as she shapes the foil into a cup.

The black gum is hard and cracked. It crumbles easily into powder and fills the foil cup.

She pours the powder into her mouth and at first thinks there is no hope for it. But on her tongue, it reforms into paste and then gum, gives her a taste of the star anise from Uruguay. She breathes through it, facing the Sea of Cortez. She chews slowly, imagining the black gum as ink, feeling it gather and reform itself. She closes her eyes and opens her palm to unveil the paper wrapper.

She opens her eyes and reads. She reads—truly reads—for the first time since the coyote passed her that scrap, that scrap confiscated with her clothes and hair. She reads, the dip into a flight. She reads:

BLACK STAR
...A taste beyond words!

She reads it aloud to the crouching hare. She flips the wrapper to see the other side, hoping for her and the hare, it's black eyes so wide and alert, ears aquiver. But there is only a trademark. She reads it anyway: blackstar™

This seems too much for the hare and it bolts. Two floating leaps and it is gone from sight. Equisa closes her eyes, chews softly, cups her ears and wonders if she's up to something. Is she gathering something? Or will she feel this way for the rest of this life, as though she must gather research and proof for her mentor, with Murrieta Tolan's lab in the Popo foothills as her perpetual return. She thinks of the letter e.

Then *ure*.

Soft thunder from the distant storm pops twice in the blue sky. It's more feeling than sound.

Twenty-six

I WOKE IN THE middle of the night with my thumb caught in the book. That had not happened to me for a long time. The last time was before I became a librarian, when I was still an undergraduate at UCLA. It still happened to Marisa. Sometimes I would find her asleep with her thumb in a book.

At first, I thought it was the book that had wakened me. My thumb was tingling, trapped as it was between the pages of *Equisa*. The room was very dark and the entire library above me felt compressed in silence, as in a power outage. Someone was standing over me. I smelled cigarettes and licorice and—before fright set in—realized it was Catalina.

"Jack," she whispered. "You might as well help me. This time. Since you're here."

She flicked her lighter and the room bloomed into shadows and soft yellow. She still wore her work dress.

"How many boxes do you have?" I asked. It was the only thing I could think to say. Dream fragments still sparked and I was caught a bit in what I had just read, was processing what was real and what was in *Equisa*. The flame of the lighter also had me thinking about the medieval monks and being with Marisa at Calafia.

Too, as I looked at Catalina in the flame light, saw how focused she was on her task, I could not help picturing Equisa as her, the way readers do with characters in order to contain them.

Cat pushed the lighter closer to the book which now lay in my lap like breakfast in bed.

"That thing," she whispered. "You're still carrying that

around? You want to bring it along? I can take care of it for you."

"It's just a book." I pushed myself into a better sitting position. The air felt cool against my bare chest.

Cat winced at the burn of the flame and had to let it go out. We were in darkness again.

"I know what it is," she replied. "Valeria told me about it. That you're still assessing it. Not a good example, Jack. To show her."

"And all those boxes," I said. I nodded toward the cart beyond the doorway, even though I knew Cat could not see in the darkness. "Would that be a good thing to show her?"

She struck the lighter right in front of my eyes, blinding me.

•

Outside the loading door, Cat had fitted that same flatbed trailer with eight book cartons. How she got the trailer here, I could only guess. She must have towed it with her car, kept it parked at her home or at a garage somewhere in Ensenada. She proficiently set the hitch and secured the boxes. I felt little more than accomplice.

"At least let me drive."

"I like the drive," she replied. She cinched a strap. "You keep watch."

"The cartons arrive during afternoon shift. How do you hide these?"

She secured the final strap, stood straight, held very still. We were working in the light of a slivered moon. She was a silhouette with burnishes of silver along the muscles of her bare arms, the contours of her collarbones. Her jaw was set and her eyes—though I could not fully discern them—were wide and black and on me.

My realization was late, behind hers for a full minute. From up the hillside, a whippoorwill sang its three notes. These cartons, though they looked the same as our assessment ones, were not the same. She had assumed I knew. We both waited for the other to speak, to play a card. I thought of the best guesses, the most extreme possibilities. She packed our dormant holdings into old assessment cartons. Or she was accepting boxes from other libraries. I guessed the latter but remained keen to the former.

"You're an outsource," I said. I moved close enough to see her expression in the moonlight, almost touching.

She raised her face to mine, her lashes slick and long.

"And," I said, her silence setting me adrift, the way you feel when you've lost your space in a book, back-treading through passages to find your way. "You're mixing in our dormants."

She put her lips to my ear, her breath cigarettes and licorice—but maybe the licorice was from my dreams.

"Burn these," she whispered, her hand on my shoulder. "Or burn the reading room."

•

I DROVE. SHE SHONE the light of her cell so that we could go faster. The cart labored more with this longer trailer and I had to make wider turns around the bend. I felt pressed to ascend as quickly and steadily as possible, sensing her passenger frustration.

"I'm already implicated," I told her. "Just by helping you like this. Keeping me in the dark doesn't protect me."

A cloud of bats whooshed overhead. She aimed her light in time to catch a glimpse of their angled, papery wings. I steered blind for a moment, resisting the impulse to slow. The surrounding brush whisked the side of the cart.

"Why do people keep writing books, Jack? Why do they

have to publish them? Why can't they just make one and stick it in someone's attic? Why can't they just *read*?"

She re-aimed her light and I took a sudden curve, just in time. Her body pressed into mine. I put my arm around her shoulders and kept her close in the straightaway.

"Why can't you toss that thing you're reading—or not reading? Just toss it into the flames?"

"I have," I said. "It keeps coming back."

"Did you bring it?"

"I left it in the burn bin. I'll take care of it tomorrow."

We were in the final stretch toward Cuervo. She turned off her light and I could see through the archway of trees and bushes and rocks that he had already been fired. A soft light glowed from his open belly flap.

"Don't worry," she explained. "I pre-heat him early." She put her hand on mine, keeping my arm around her shoulders. "When you visit Cisco," she said. "Do you ever walk through his little house? He only keeps a few books, a small shelf in every room, even the kitchen. But they always change. Almost month to month. Only a couple stay. He likes Cortázar and Camus."

I eased the cart and trailer onto the plateau and parked. Looking over Ensenada and the dark Pacific, we sat like teenagers.

"Maybe he's the last cronopio," I said.

"I don't remember what a cronopio is," she said. "It's been so long since I read Cortázar. I didn't know there was supposed to be a last one."

"There isn't," I said. "It's just something from that thing we're not reading. It's supposedly the last book ever made of paper. That's just the title. *The Last Cronopio*."

In the glow from the city below, I could see her thinking, recalling, flipping through pages.

"In the Cortázar book," she said. "Weren't they naïve but very imaginative creatures? Small, shifty. But outside the book—for him in real life—cronopios were thinkers and creators. Innocent, free, outside of things. Louie Armstrong was the first cronopio."

"It was just a word he invented," I replied. "Without definition."

Behind us, Cuervo hissed. His heat grazed our necks. Below, the lights of Ensenada spilled into the sea.

She asked about finding the books in Tijuana, about the condition of the bins. I told her the good and bad, that one could eventually find a book and that it would be in decent shape. But that at least one entire bin was missing, most likely dumped into the sea, that possibly our books were being used as a front. I described the barrels but she did not appear interested in that part.

She tilted her head away from me as she mused over the cityscape. Her neck caught the moonlight, hollows forming beneath ear and jaw. Our dreams, for the most part, had come true. Somewhere along our careers and relationships, they had passed into reality. We had nothing to complain about, nothing to write. We knew going in that being a librarian meant learning the art of receiving, the contours of acceptance, the nuance between holding and withholding.

The sea was the blackest part of our view, the sky lit by moon and stars and the upward push of the city. With the sudden motionless of spilled ink, it marked up and down the Baja coast, stretches of undulation jagged by sawtooth cliffs.

Cuervo expanding sounded a metal clang.

"He's ready," said Catalina.

•

SHE WAS EXPERT AT jackknifing the trailer in front of Cuervo's belly. I rolled up my sleeves and she re-did her hair, tight and back against any danger of singeing. Her expression was hard, the look of a stoker already in mid-shift. She did not enjoy this.

She cut the seal of the first carton and opened the flaps. I could see that she had mixed the contents. Some of the books were fresh assessments, some had Deweys on their spines. Some were hardly books any more, their plates frayed, quires sliding free or missing.

She motioned for me to gather the first armload. I hefted ten and waited for her. She put her hands on her hips.

"Anyone who wants to start writing a book should have to do this first," she declared. "Anyone who wants to publish them should have to do this for a month."

She was best at this and I was second. Valeria, no doubt, would eventually pass me. Together we were a machine, alternating armloads, timing our heaves into the flames. Our backs ached by the third carton and we exchanged looks as we paused to stretch. Her skin shimmered with sweat, her dress pulled to her thighs. We never stopped to read even one sentence.

Twenty-seven

JUST AS FLACO PREDICTED, the southern swell arrived. Brigadoons grew too big for amateurs. All I could do with my sunrises was swim dashes in the rough breakwater then sit on shore and watch the experts ride giants. Even with the pros out there, Flaco was the best, the one the others watched from the lineup. He claimed waves others feared, would send the lineup flailing. His drops looked almost like falls, everyone thinking he leaned too far forward, but his arms remained steady, as though calming the water. When the wave was spent and shouldering, he would bail out, fly over the lip, a lone figure against the morning sky.

This first March swell lasted three days, taking me to Sunday. I burned one more trailer of books with Catalina at night and one more bin with Valeria at noon. I lost track of *Equisa*. Admittedly, it was a passive move on my part. I had lied to Cat when I told her I had left it in the burn bin. Not knowing what I wanted to do with it, I had placed it in the conservation room, among about a dozen books designated for minor repairs. When it was my turn in the rotation to conduct repairs, *Equisa* was no longer in the stack. I didn't ask any of the others about it.

Catalina and I did not examine the books we burned. I could tell just by feel and weight that some were old and some were new. Some of the old felt light and powdery, handfuls of moth wings. Some of the new hadn't even been cracked open, neat and slick as a fresh deck of cards. Cuervo's fire would blind us to the surrounding night, our eyes adjusted to the near flame. We worked alone in a white-hot bubble of light, aloft in utter darkness.

With Valeria, it was different. With the daylight and the EPL-labeled burn bin, we could be dutiful. Though she liked to sometimes pause and smirk over a rejected assessment, we both showed each other the spent classics, the broken and worn volumes that had to be replaced due to overuse. As she held a copy of *Tess of the D'Urbervilles*, whole quires missing like rotted teeth, I told her that it never got easy, that, yes, you will always feel you are incinerating those favorite sentences. But afterward, maybe during re-stacking, when you come across a title you could recall burning, you will feel a temporary sense of accomplishment, a gardener after weeding. But there was no accurate analogy for what a librarian does. It is a wholly unique position, defined by an endless series of contradictory decisions and actions, inhabited in a space formed by human whim and aspiration.

"Celebrated by fire," she added.

That Sunday, I had to take Valeria along with me for my regular visit with Cisco. Our tour at the San Diego annex was scheduled for that afternoon and I wanted to make the most of my time with Cisco. I also wanted to give Valeria a chance to get to know him better, to see him away from the EPL. I felt it my duty. And I feared her odd mix of aggression and respect in her regard for books.

•

CISCO HAD AN EXTRA chair ready for Valeria. He brought out more potato chips and lime, iced the beer in a leaky wooden bucket. The melted ice seeped over the pale clay tiles in cloud-like patterns. Valeria removed her sandals and, with her toe, led the water into desired shapes. The wind off the bay was soft. The kitchen radio played a ranchera station, just audible through the open patio door.

Cisco had spent his vacation time walking the 1900 miles of the Baja shoreline. He would do this in segments, stretches that grew shorter as he grew older. Until now, he explained to Valeria, when he would just wander the beaches, retracing bits of past excursions. When she asked, he told her he didn't take photos.

He held up a waiting hand then left us to go find something inside. Valeria looked at me as though she were about to ask several questions, leaning forward, lips parted, hands gripping chair. But she remained silent.

I told her that Cisco really did know every title in our holdings. I told her to think about it. How he would want to walk the most varied coastline in the world, one formed by mountain, ocean, and desert, where plants and animals changed with every micro-climate waiting beyond the next outcrop. How this must free his mind, expand his memory with impossibility.

"Did he ever take anyone with him?" she asked. The question made me feel old, her concern for that, her automatic aim toward loneliness.

I told her that sometimes he had people meet him along the way, but that they would only hike brief stretches with Cisco before parting. There was a woman from La Paz, a librarian there, who served as his first guide on the Sea of Cortez side.

"Were they lovers?" she asked.

"Of sorts," I answered, again feeling a splinter of age. It was when he was young, just starting to really cultivate the EPL and its holdings. "Way before my time," I said.

Cisco returned carrying a very old pair of leather boots and a tin contraption that looked like a boy's science project. He placed these on the coffee table, arranging them on either side of the chip plate. The boots were curled and dry, their soles and laces gone. They looked like things that would expand and normalize when dropped in water.

"This was my first pair," Cisco told us. "The only ones I still have. I had them resoled in La Paz. Ten times, always at the same cobbler."

"Boots," said Valeria. "I was picturing you walking barefoot on the beach."

He explained that most of the hiking was rugged, especially on the ocean side. But you needed boots on the Cortez side, too, because of the heat and the snakes and scorpions. "And the jumping *chollas*," he added.

I could see Valeria thinking hard about jumping *chollas*.

"It's just a kind of cactus," I said.

"That doesn't make it sound any better," she replied.

With the tip of her middle finger, she touched the tin contraption, as though testing for heat.

"That was his first desalinizing kit," I said.

I explained how he built it himself, that he got it from a how-to book written by a Japanese soldier who had been abandoned on an island during World War II.

"You drank ocean water," she said. She looked at Cisco as though he were an undersea dweller, come ashore to visit humans.

"It's the only water around," I said. "For most of the time."

I could tell her these things because I had been sharing these monthly Sundays with Cisco for seventeen years. After most visits, I came away feeling we had spoken very little, exchanged almost nothing more than soccer talk. With Valeria here, I suddenly felt both empty and brimming. I worried that I had accomplished nothing past the age of thirty-four, but felt somehow ready, on this tranquil patio overlooking the *bahía*. But ready for what, I could not sense. I was now happy I had brought Valeria, almost forgetting where we were headed.

She gazed at the water.

"I haven't spotted a whale yet," she said. "Since moving here. Everybody tells me they're out there. Everybody tells me how to do it."

Neither Cisco nor I told her you couldn't see them from here. We let her look. Only lost whales ventured into the *bahía*. It happened once every few years. They usually got named because they appeared so cordial, the way they nosed around the hulls of the navy ships. The last one was a male named *Payaso* because he looked like a clown with an X over one eye and a rim of orange sea lice along his upper lip.

With frank expression, Valeria turned to Cisco first, then me, then to the water. "I know there won't be any in the bay. I know you have to spot them over open sea. And I know the season is ending. If not over."

She twirled a bottle of beer in the ice bucket, gathered thoughts, something that brought the wavering curve of a smile to her lips. She told us about grays, some things we knew. They migrate from the Bering Sea to the Baja lagoons every year, 14,000 miles round trip. They mate and calve in the lagoons. Their gestation period supposedly fits perfectly into this pattern, but sometimes the calves come early and the mothers give birth along the way, off the California coast.

We call it migration but that's just us not understanding the other. Three months in the arctic waters, three months traveling south, three months of having sex and lolling in the lagoons, three months traveling back north. But using a different route, an open sea passage.

They feed on the ocean floor. They have to lie on their

sides and bite and filter. Usually their right side, but a few use their left—yes, left-handed whales. We can tell because the side that scrapes the ocean floor gets scarred in a certain way. Some of the older ones lose that eye.

She looked at Cisco. He was watching the bay. She aligned her view with his, sipped her beer.

We say they have a language, that they call to one another across hundreds of miles. We say they sing. But we just don't recognize the other, accept the other. She told us she liked to imagine that some of the whales would have to be assigned as librarians, tasked to hold all the stories and narratives from all the migrations. "Maybe that's what we're hearing when we capture their songs," she said. "Their card catalogues."

"Did you know?" she asked us. "That we can measure their population density by comparing their song pitch? Lower pitch equals more whales. Higher pitch equals declining population. Our logic figures that higher pitch travels longer, covers the increased spread due to decline. But why do we do that? Say they sing?" She fashioned finger quotes, beer still in hand. "But then don't credit them with the nature of song. Wonder if the pitch changes because life changes."

The three of us gazed at the lifeless bay, metallic under noon sun.

"Still," said Valeria. "I have yet to spot one."

"You can go down to Scammon's Lagoon on a weekend," I told her. "See dozens right from the shore."

"I don't want to see them that way. First. I want to see them alone out there in the open sea. Cold and urgent. I want to see one that might have broken from the pod, to cool off, get some perspective."

She eyed Cisco. "They do that you know."

Cisco had remained silent during the whale talk. Finally,

he responded to her. “Our library alone has 9,321 titles on whales. We probably mean very little to the leviathans. Tiny specks peeking at them from distant shores. Poking at them from a distant surface. Curiosities. How many sounds do you think they could have for us?”

“Two.” Valeria sipped her beer, tapped the bottle tip to her chin. “One for threat. One for irrelevant.”

“Maybe one more,” he replied. “For something we can't know.”

I wondered if I could convince Valeria to skip the annex tour, to stay here a while longer, drink as many beers as we wanted, and in doing so, convince myself. But I knew Cisco would not approve, that he wanted us to meet our obligations. He had taught Catalina and me that obeying the North allowed us to thrive down here. So instead, I reminded myself to plan a camping trip to Scammon's, to pitch a tent between the dunes and the shore and see the grays in the morning. Sometimes you could hear their huffs in the night.

I hadn't done that since before my divorce. Marisa was always with me at Scammon's. We'd marvel at how the lagoon slid easily into the desert landscape, calm and shallow. Under a full moon was best, the dunes and water reflecting the light with the same brightness and tone. And then I worried, sitting there between Cisco and Valeria, if I would be able to go alone. Would I be able to face that openness, that sense of permanence heightened by the occasional whale's breech? When you see them in the lagoons, you can't help seeing that, their wallowing in this return.

Twenty-eight

We stopped along a low cliff near Rosarito. I wanted Valeria to spot a gray. The afternoon sun was not ideal, but this point was one of the best for viewing the migration. She was more nervous about the time than I.

"We'll be late," she said.

"Not very," I replied. "We can blame the border."

We walked to the edge of the overlook. She positioned herself facing slightly north, visored her hand over her eyes and scanned the ocean. She stood slightly tiptoe. I used binoculars, dividing the expanse into contained circles, inching my way south to north, against the grain of the whales' journey. Even this late in the migration, I felt confident. I felt the opposite about the EPL. I marked my spot along the horizon, eased the binoculars away, and rested my eyes.

Even though she appeared focused on the water, I sensed anxiousness from Valeria, a furtive incline to her shoulders. The ocean breeze wrapped her sundress about her.

"If we don't leave soon..."

"We'll leave after we spot one," I said. "We'll be fine."

"We can't be late." She looked at me, her hand still visored. "I can't be late."

"Who do you work for?" I resumed my search, covering my eyes with the binoculars.

"What do you mean?"

My circle of vision was calm, the ocean beyond the swells smooth, free of white-caps and good for spotting. It helped me to focus on that surface, imagine the depths, how the undersea sun would glow as pale as the moon.

She yanked my arm, pulling the binoculars away, forcing me to face her. I expected her expression to be defiant. But it was one of hurt.

I tried to explain. "The state of California stopped funding its libraries years ago. But they still control disbursement. That's the worst kind of power—clerical power. The crummy kid who owns the only good soccer ball, so he gets to play and say when the game's over. You think I'm down here under-achieving. With Cat and Cisco. But we run a library. A serviceable library."

"What do you think I am?" she asked.

"Spy, saboteur, or exile," I answered. "Probably a mix. I'm not sure I care."

"It's different for me." The breeze blew her short hair over to one side and across her face. "Different than it was for you. Than it is for you. You get to be what you wanted to be. I know you all have your prices to pay. I know that. But for you the tide ebbs and flows. The shore that's left is different but the same—each time."

She aimed her look to the ocean, resumed her search, tiptoe. "I am all three of those things you said. I'm all three so I can be one. A librarian. Maybe the last librarian."

"I'm sorry," I told her.

"They tell me how you go around the world visiting libraries, big and small." She appeared more focused now on her task, jaw set, shoulders even. "But have you visited an empty one yet? No books, no readers? Big, small. Loved, forgotten. It doesn't matter. When you see those empty shelves and empty chairs, it feels the same. You feel like the last librarian."

"I felt that way once," I replied. "The last time I visited the Palafox in Puebla. It was the first public library in the New World. It has a beautiful reading room. It has 45,000 books.

Almost all of them are in dead languages. No one was there. The books weren't even visible. A caretaker was polishing the floors. No librarian. Every time I went back, no matter what time of day, what day of the week, it was the same. When I set up tours, the guides never showed and it was always only me and that guy polishing the floors."

"That's not what I meant," she said. "But, okay."

"You mean the ones that gave up and gutted themselves."

"Yes. Those."

"There will always be books, Valeria."

"So we're told." She shaded her eyes with both hands, thumbs to ears. "But I don't believe it. And neither do you."

A school of dolphins came into my circle of vision, their dorsal fins arcing over the surface in a play of rhythms and patterns. I let her find them.

"Oh," she said.

I offered her the binoculars, nudging them to her shoulder so she could keep the school in her sights. As I tracked her line, I saw the gray. Beyond and behind the dolphins, its spout fired a cloud of water that broke apart quickly in the breeze. My heart flipped. Every time, that happened. This time it was stronger.

"To your right and a little back," I whispered, as though that mattered.

She adjusted her line, kept the binoculars steady. "I don't see anything."

"Just keep looking there, outside the dolphins. It'll breathe a few more times, gathering air for a dive. Keep looking," I told her.

I looked away from the water. I watched her profile as she peered through the binoculars. She bit her lower lip and kept steady watch. I could tell she hadn't spotted anything.

"It's a unique spout." I spoke softly, as though not to disturb the delicate view. "They have two holes, so the plume is doubled. Like a heart. Higher than you think."

Worry creased her temple. Her fingers shifted slightly along the binoculars. Maybe the only thing better than seeing that whale at that moment, would be to see Valeria spot one for the first time. I imagined a momentary return to innocence for both of us.

Her lips parted. Her dark eyes widened. I could see the ocean reflected there, compressed by the lens into a blue disc. And I knew she saw it. And I knew she would watch it surface again and again until it finally had enough air to take below the surface for an unimaginable span of time. It's gone, she would say. But it was there.

Twenty-nine

THE ANNEX WAS A converted blimp hangar on the desert outskirts of San Diego. Inside, it was a hundred feet to the rafters. The humidity and temperature controls were solar powered. No one really needed to be there. As long as the sun rose over the southern California desert, it could run itself indefinitely. Visiting aliens could discover it hundreds of years after our demise, books organized and preserved. They could learn the annexed version of our culture.

Anyone considering writing a book, publishing a book, should be required to visit such a place. All major libraries around the world, public as well as university, had them. Every annex that I knew of resided in some kind of converted building, internal floors gutted to provide pure vertical space. Old prisons and asylums were the most popular choices, buildings that contained too many ghosts.

This one used the Harvard model which was fast becoming the global standard for organization and storage. A small staff ran the front room, taking in the books, assigning and recording shelf space. Though the volumes still bore Deweys on their spines, they were located according to size. A very simple measuring board was used, a two-foot square of plywood with five sizing rectangles. The rectangles were painted atop one another. Green, red, black, yellow, blue. Green, the smallest, was the size of a hardcover novel. Blue, the largest, was the size of a modest coffee table book.

An arrival was simply laid atop the measuring board, assigned whichever color came close to fitting, then shelved alongside others of the same color classification. This allowed for maximizing space. It was what a lot of people did with their books at home. Shelve them according to how evenly they fit, eschewing any regard for alphabet, author, theme, value, or era. Until requested, they were just geometric blocks.

The stacks were breathtaking. They ran the height of the building and the length of the floor. The space between was just wide enough to allow for a compact cherry-picker to run up and down the aisles. Just standing in an aisle, one was overcome by the upward sheer, the overwhelming sense of amount.

This annex held three million volumes with room for a million more. Each aisle had two stacks, one on each side, a hundred feet high. Each stack was divided vertically into ladders, each ladder divided into rungs of shelves. When you entered the book's Dewey, you received five numbers: aisle, stack, ladder, shelf, book. 4-2-7-98-23 would be the twenty-third book on a shelf almost a hundred feet up on ladder seven.

The cherry-pickers rolled like robots up and down the aisles. They lifted you up to that shelf a hundred feet high so you could pluck free that requested volume. But whenever I was on one of these tours, I would wonder at those two words—*requested volume*. It was pointless to ask how many requests were received, because the response was almost certain to be a lie, some reconfigured value meant to prove validation. Even Catalina lied—to me—when asked about our dormants.

In a room full of three million books available free to millions of patrons, requests should steadily arrive. But in all my annex tours, I never once saw one of those robot cherry-pickers fetch a book. I only ever saw them shelve a new arrival. I broke from a tour and camped out in the San Francisco annex for an entire day and observed this.

I did believe requests happened. But whenever I stood between the vast and dizzying aisles of one of these annexes, I felt—at best—to be in the Valley of Unwanted Books. At worst, I felt that almost all books eventually became unwanted and that I was standing at the bottom of literary Hell, where useless books were tortured with the faint promise of being caressed.

I did my best during this tour. I believed in professional accreditation. I liked that librarians were required to continually learn and adapt, that even though common perception pegged us as dowdy and conservative, we most likely participated in one of the most dynamic of professions. That was our secret. We were superheroes in disguise.

I took notes and asked sincere questions. I did ask what happened to all the blimps, but only because I knew the director wanted to give us a brief history of the building. I volunteered to take a ride on one of the cherry-pickers. The guide and I were given a book's five-sequence number. We rolled down to the far end of an aisle and then we were lifted eighty-three shelves high. The sense of amount was even more intense from that height, the aisle floors like thin ribbons between the stacks, the tour group like model railroad figurines, miniature librarians awaiting transport.

I selected the correctly numbered book from the shelf and we descended. We rolled up the aisle to greet the others, book in hand. Of course, it was a false retrieval, to be returned to its place after the tour was over, to forever await a genuine request. A 1958 amateur study of the larks and pipits of Denmark. I surreptitiously peeked at one sentence. "After morning tea, I woke Mikkel by tapping a wooden spoon to his broad forehead."

During all of this, Valeria was gone. I had expected this.

We parted upon arrival. Her only remark was that we were both underdressed. I assured her that this was okay. We represented the Ensenada Public Library. Her sundress looked better than anything else I could see and I had a tie in the back pocket of my jeans. When she moved to apologize, took a step back from the director who was leading her, I turned away.

Thirty

On our return, Valeria asked that we stop at the same overlook near Rosarito, where we had spotted the Pacific gray. It was night, with nothing to see but a thin moon over a shadowy sea. The water looked black until it met the sheer and utter darkness of the cliffs. Below us, the sound of the waves was rhythmical, each swell going through its crest, crash, and hiss over the sand before the next arrived.

The breeze was cool and a little misty. I gave her a towel from the car and she wrapped it about her shoulders as a shawl. I considered putting my arm around her, not as any kind of overture, only as an act of camaraderie, one soldier to another. I wanted to let her know that I understood that she despised the tour as much as I did, that it was an expression of power, that our roles—though different—demanded sublimation and appreciation, awe.

Her face was pale. Her sinewy posture appeared precarious, verging on some kind of release. And I only now thought to ask if she'd eaten.

"Did they offer you food?"

"Only those sandwiches," she replied. "Probably the same they offered you."

"I never take their food."

"Me neither," she said. "It's like Hades."

I laughed. "I always think that, too."

"But we always have to go back, anyway," she said. "Right? We're Persephone whether or not we eat."

"If you need," I offered. "We can head back to Rosarito. There are good places still open there."

"Thanks, no." She opened her arms to let the night breeze into the towel, then re-wrapped herself. "This is good."

I took in some air, tasted the mist. I let Baja take its effect on her, the precipice, the sublime crash below, the feel that you were somehow standing in the sky. She broke a little.

"I didn't sell you out completely, you know." She rolled her shoulders beneath the towel, a squirm in a cocoon. "I said a lot of good things, too. Things they would want to hear."

"How much did you tell them?"

"I told them about the day books you take to the incinerator." She almost turned to look at me but kept her eyes on the black ocean. "But not about the night ones. I fudged a little. Said you were throwing extras in with the assessment. But I didn't say anything about what you might be doing at night. You and Cat and whoever else plays in the basement with you."

"Did they make you an offer?"

She barely hesitated. "Not yet."

"When they do," I said. "When they deem your exile over, your price paid. Think about staying down here anyway."

"Like you did?"

"Not like me. I did it for that." I nodded toward the ocean. "I just think that the EPL will outlast all of theirs. So, if you want to be the last librarian."

"I don't want to be that. I don't want to be that woman in that book."

I looked at her, traced her line of vision to the open water. "How far have you read?"

"Further than you." She glanced at me, settled back to the water, but closer in, where the breakers flashed white crests. "I read past your dog ear. You left her on top of that hill, with that hare. Overlooking Guaymas and the Sea of Cortez. Reading a gum wrapper like it was Jane Austen."

She gathered the towel tightly about her shoulders. "You want to know what I told them."

"Not really," I replied. "I figure that if we handle everything they send us, they'll look the other way. North."

"They had me design stacks. Using our reading room."

"Right there?" I asked. "On the spot?"

She shook her head and smiled. "I can't figure if you're way behind or way ahead. Like the woman in the book. No, not on the spot." She let the towel fall from her shoulders and shivered. "I have them on my phone. I have designs that have low stacks replacing the tables. And I have some that fill the room top to bottom. Like an annex."

I feigned disinterest, but shivered, imagining our reading room filled ceiling to floor with organized, numbered pulp. "They know we burn books. We've used Cuervo for decades to take care of discards and damages."

"They have no idea how many we burn," she replied.

Do you? I wanted to ask her. But I felt vulnerable, that I might spill more than she. With the 1600 per week Catalina was feeding Cuervo on the side added to the official 2000 assessments per week, we were burning near 200,000 a year. Still, that was not even close to stemming the flow.

I thought of Equisa on that hill in Guaymas, atop the Witch's Hat, reading the gum wrapper, amused by the hare, worried about what she sensed coming over the Sea of Cortez. She was heading our way. From Guaymas, you crossed the narrow sea to the center of the eastern shore of Baja.

"Where is it?" I asked, wondering if Valeria was on the same page.

She lifted herself toward the sea, parted her lips to answer. Then caught herself with a laugh. "I thought you meant that whale we saw. You mean *Equisa*. Your ex has it. I caught her poking around the burn bin. She told me what she was looking for and I gave it to her. It's the most popular book in the EPL and it isn't even registered. In fact, technically it's burned."

"Did you two have fun at my expense?"

"Sure we did. A little. Mainly we talked about the book. She told me you read it to her. Left her hanging."

She focused on the ocean, but smiled thoughtfully, inwardly. In little increments, she turned her shoulders side to side. "Marisa seemed quite at home in the basement."

We stood abreast listening to the steady surf. Not often did the sets arrive this way, neatly measured, each wave allowed its full course before the next washed over it. And in the darkness below, it was all sound to us. And we gave our thoughts to it, to the one-two-three of it, the initial slap of the crest, the crash of the break, and the hush over the shore. The third lasted longest, with the most variation as it rinsed across the sand, finding new lengths, different arcs. In each, we thought of sentences we had read and wanted to read again.

Thirty-one

I HADN'T PLANNED ON spending yet another night in the EPL. But after I dropped off Valeria there and watched her drive away, I felt very alone. Going to my house promised nothing but more loneliness. The library at night at least offered the possibility of solitude.

On the bed lay *Equisa*. Not centered or propped, but tossed, the bedcover rippled. I noted three bookmarks. My dog ear—yes, a library sin. Beyond that, Valeria's torn strip of paper. On this, I penciled the letters *u-r-e* and returned it to its crease. The third was a small feather, seagull gray with a black tip. This one, Marisa's, was nearing the end.

I read to catch up and to find my way to sleep.

•

AFTER THIRTY PAGES, I was still awake. I had passed Valeria and was nearing Marisa's feather. When I sensed that Equisa might be on the verge of retrieving the corner scrap, I had to read even further:

> From her perch atop the Witch's Hat, she assesses the docks. In neat wooden lines out and across, they form giant letters over the water, letters from another alphabet, capital *Ts* and *Fs* with extra crosslines, *Ms* and *Ns* with extra links and diagonals. She leaves the nostalgic comfort of the sitting stone and descends.
>
> She imagines the momentum of the descent carries her through the bustle of Guaymas and in a moment she is at the docks. Up close she sees the wood is not real. The slats are composed of conglomerates molded from

materials rendered in quarries. She is sad for her cousin. Ferrymen on the closest docks spot her and begin to position themselves. They pretend to do things—secure the ties, polish their rails, toggle their booms—all while leaning toward Equisa, showing her that this boat is best, this one is fastest, this one glides smooth. She sees them trying to figure her, figure what she needs.

Because she likes the odd letter it forms on the water, she steps onto a dock shaped like a *Z* on a stick. Three ferrymen from this dock immediately begin to approach her. They glance at the water as they approach, eye the gulls overhead, the pelicans perched on rails, tap the cells in their hands. One ferryman, his boat docked in the middle of the *Z*'s diagonal, stays back. He just looks at her. She counts past twenty and he is still gazing at her, unwavering. She can feel it, herself being read.

She muscles through the group of ferrymen. They tug at her forearms, pull her elbows, grab her shoulders. They offer prices, best one another, promise speed and comfort and wonderful sights, smooth sailing.

As soon as she clears their initial grasps, she turns to face all of them, their hands still reaching for another try at her. She is able to see them all at once, glare at them all. She does this by choosing one pair of eyes and boring her gaze into them. The other two ferrymen see this, see their rival struck in her gaze, see him being read. Their glances flick between the gulls, the pelicans, and the beam of Equisa's stare. Beneath them, the *Z*-shaped dock pitches softly from small, almost imperceptible waves rolling in from the distant storm over the Sea of Cortez.

They fall back and Equisa walks toward the ferryman who stands in the very middle of the *Z*. His boat, which bobs beside him, is green and white and smaller than the others. The bundled sails look like crumpled parchment. Maybe, she thinks, small means fast, the colors will be elusive on the open sea, the sails are old because they are good.

I feared I would have to wait too long, he says to her as she nears. He is at ease on the bobbing dock. He is short, with broad heavy shoulders. His arms and face are very dark. He smiles as he holds her gaze and his teeth are large and white. And even though they do not look at all like the slanted teeth of Julio Guzman, they remind her of the coyote.

Puzzled by his words, she asks how much to cross the sea. He gives her the price and then hops onto his boat to retrieve something. He digs inside the hull. She hears him move things aside, push and slide panels, the way she sometimes sees Murrieta Tolan search for paper and quires she has hidden away.

The ferryman hops back to the dock, vaulting the rail as though on a playground. He swings a canvas bag. He hands this bag to her. His black hair sweeps in curls across his face, partially obscuring his grin, his big white teeth.

These are from Julio, he tells her. Sent by Julio.

The bag holds her clothes, the ones the woman in the DEA windbreaker had taken from her in the Chihuahua desert.

That's not possible, she replies. Julio Guzman died.

He tells her that Julio had taken precautions to secure her route, that he had inside help. He tells her they will have to hurry, that the storm might bring waterspouts and that most likely these clothes were being chased.

He helps her over the rail and onto the boat by simply

offering his arm. His arm is hard as driftwood.

Onboard, Equisa unfolds the jeans and checks the coin pocket, where she had last tucked the scrap. At first, it feels empty. But as she worms her finger deeper, she realizes the paper has blended into the softness of the cloth. She thinks of vellum again, paper made of skin. The thieves, not knowing how paper sometimes reverts toward its source, missed it.

She smooths the scrap into her palm, keeping it in her shadow, protected from the bleaching rays of the sun. She offers the ferryman a look, a good read. Together they take in the letters: *ure*.

The ferryman offers a grateful smile and begins untying the sails. Equisa can see by his inward expression—on such an open face!—that he is still going over those three letters, that he is still in that last act of reading, that moment of venture beyond the words. His sad look remains even as he smiles, his fingers quick on the sail ties.

She asks him why he is sad and he tells her that now he is sure Julio is gone, but that he also knows at least his quest is still alive.

Is he buried in a nice place? he asks.

She tells him, yes, and that it is marked with his name in a desert hollow that floods with moonlight. She tells him that Julio, with his last breaths, had saved her life and saved a book.

The ferryman nods and then hoists the sails. The boat strains against its ties, the ropes tightening around the dock cleats.

I need to get to Baja and the Guadalupe Valley, Equisa says to the ferryman. I have cousins there. Then I can get up to the border and find the rest of the book.

He looks skeptical, eyes the scrap in her hand.

I can do that, she tells him. Believe it. The way I believe you can get me across the water, through tornadoes and whoever might be chasing.

Waterspouts, he corrects. Not tornadoes.

She folds the scrap into the Black Star gum wrapper and tucks this into the coin pocket of the jeans she is wearing. She gives the bag of clothes back to the ferryman and he secures two big fishing weights to it and tosses it overboard. She watches the bundle sink, the veil of bubbles that form on the green surface.

With the sails slacked to the wind, he is able to release the dock lines from the cleats. He shows Equisa where to sit to avoid the swing of the boom and gives her some water. He asks that she serve as lookout. She agrees though does not exactly know what that entails.

They set sail and swiftly get to open sea, using the wind coming from the storm to outrun the storm. Mexico, to the east, is a thin line of desert. Baja, to the west, lies beyond the horizon. To the north, their primary direction, the island of Tiburon appears to constantly float away from them. The sea is a lighter blue than the sky. Low, thin clouds break free ahead of the storm.

Those will bring waterspouts, says the ferryman, pointing to the wisps overhead.

Equisa is struck by his certainty, by the way he speaks as he works the wheel and the swing of the boom. When he notices her looking ahead, he tells her to scan the other direction. She spots three sails on the horizon. Far away, she tells him. Three but far away.

He immediately swings the wheel, the mainsail popping, and they pick up speed but in another direction. They can't possibly catch us, she says. They're using the same wind.

He laughs, showing his big teeth again. She realizes he must be Julio Guzman's cousin, at heart if not blood. Like her, he is acting on legacy. He is *Primo Equis*.

Those are faster boats, he tells her.

How can sailboats race? she asks. The wind is the wind.

He laughs more and wags his shaggy head. When she looks back, the three sails have gained on them. She can see the pale hulls, how they cut the water into white feathers.

The chase became my favorite part of the book and the main reason I was unable to find my way to sleep. In my reclined position on the basement bed, I felt somewhat laid out and struck. I adjusted my pillow, flexed my neck and continued, venturing back in with the last images still in my head. The three boats neared and Equisa could see how much bigger they were than the ferry. Their tilt over the water made them appear angry and focused. All for a corner scrap of paper containing a three-letter word fragment.

She sees that the two outside boats are getting ready to flank them. She still cannot figure how they change directions in the wind, the same wind that pushes all of them northward. It all looks hopeless to her. She thinks of throwing the paper into the sea, to make a show of it so that their pursuers might stop.

The ferryman does not let her do this. Instead, he tells her to watch for waterspouts. When she looks skyward, he says, no, look at the water. He explains how they will begin on the surface of the sea, that they will look like silver coins on the blue water. When Equisa hesitates and wrinkles her brow, the ferryman waves her in close, one hand on the wheel, one cupped for her. She eases her shoulder into this hand, arches her look.

He speaks in a calm tone as he keeps his eyes on the sea, his voice low and pocketed against the wind and salt spray. He explains waterspouts to her and she feels as though she is in apex, the still gather above a waterfall. First, he tells her that he often paints them, using sheets of scrap metal from boat hulls as his canvas. That he loves to paint them but that he can never render them as well as he wanted.

Then he explains. They are not tornadoes and they will form in fair weather like this.

They begin on the surface of the ocean, he tells her. Opposing wind currents collide into a spin just above the water. The air and water molecules rotate like an upside-down drain creating friction and static that gather more air and water. The spin below starts the spin above, on the cloud's thin belly, the static electricity acting as magnet. The blossoming spout creates and increases its own energy, whirling fast enough to lift the sea, pull down the clouds.

He explains this as he steers the ferry and scans the sea. He only looks ahead, trusting Equisa to keep watch on their pursuers. She knows he tells her all of this to calm and distract her, himself as well, as though they were working together beneath the soft light of a lamp. It works and she quickly spots her first waterspout, a spinning coin of seafoam off their starboard bow.

She finds reassurance in this quiet lesson, even as the big sails bear down on them. And instantly she begins to see the coins on the water, spinning silver discs on the blue. One, two, then three. And she points and the ferryman gnashes his teeth into a grin as he swings their boat toward the burgeoning spouts.

The spouts grow quickly. They do not form top to bottom or bottom to top. Rather, they blossom as those spinning coins on the water, and then those are matched by spinning coins on the bellies of the low thin clouds, clouds that don't even block the sun. And then the two appear to grow toward each other, the cloud mist dropping down, the ocean mist rising, all swirling very fast. A cascade forms at the base of each spout, a tumbling churn of water lifted and dropped. The waterspouts are white ropes tying ocean to sky, twisting, almost looping. They are as loud as waterfalls and they cut wakes as sharply as sailboats.

The ferryman is not afraid of them, not even the biggest ones that have trunks wider than his boat. He steers very close. Equisa can feel their wind, believes she could reach her hand inside. The ferryman weaves between the spouts. He uses them to elude the pursuers who seem very reluctant to venture near the columns. It is as though the ferry escapes into a forest of water trees.

Equisa nearly swoons with the contrast, the violent churn and swirl of the spouts atop the even surface of the sea. The ferryman draws close enough to the spouts to use their tangent wind, snapping his mainsail back and forth, hurling them northward.

The way their pursuers steer clear and drop back makes her wonder if Julio Guzman's cousin is crazy, as crazy as Julio had been when he saved her from the thieves. Books make us crazy, she wonders. Maybe she is crazy.

•

I found sleep by re-reading the ferryman's explanation of the waterspouts, ear-marking my place, and imagining the scene. The dark library loomed over me. The ferryman informed Equisa on the formation of fair weather spouts.

I closed my eyes and let my head sink into the pillow. I recalled waterspouts I had seen. They occurred off the Baja coast during early spring and late fall. I would see one or two a year, usually while sitting atop my board, looking out for the next swell. I had only ever seen them at a distance, miles out, beyond the whales.

I imagined Equisa and the ferryman weaving their way between the whirling columns, catching the edges of their wind, weaving across the Sea of Cortez like a pinball through spinners. I imagined the mist on their faces, the roar of the cascades. I brought them into my dreams.

Thirty-two

I WOKE TO THE sounds of someone doing light work. At first, I thought it was Marisa making breakfast in the kitchen of our old house. Eyes still closed, I smelled coffee and felt the yellow light of morning and the softness of curtains billowed by a sea breeze. A hard sadness thumped me fully awake when I realized where I was, opened my eyes to the grayness of the library apartment.

Someone, most likely Catalina, was working in the conservation room. It was very early. The sun hadn't risen. Sleep-deprived, I almost cried.

I put on board shorts and a T-shirt and walked barefoot to the conservation room. Catalina, dressed for work, hair up, was sketching. The coffee was real. She had made a pot, enough for both of us.

She did not look up from her work, brushing a charcoal stick over paper.

"You've been hogging the bed." She paused the charcoal. "Of late."

"Sorry." My voice felt scratchy, salty. "You can have it next."

"It's okay," she replied. "I think you need it more than I."

She lifted her mug of coffee and with it motioned to the pot. "Help yourself."

"Why?" I asked as I poured myself a mug. "Why do you say that?"

She resumed her sketching, cocking her head to gain an angle. "I keep finding Marisa down here. Different times of the day, poking around, hoping to catch you, but also relieved to not find you. You need to meet. Talk to her. Reckon things out."

Catalina was right. And I tried not to resent her for it. Sketching like that, she appeared peaceful, the opposite of how she looked when we burned books together in the night. Marisa probably needed to end things with me. Did she want to? was the question.

"That Flaco guy, too," said Catalina.

I drew next to her, but giving her elbow room, not interrupting her work.

"Flaco?"

"He's moving," she told me. "To Peru. Maybe just for the winter swells there. But probably for good."

"He told you this?"

"I found him down here, too. People seem to try to find you down here." Finally, she turned to me, studied my face. "I think maybe he caught some trouble in Baja."

As though preparing to sketch, she continued to study me. "It's opposite down there, you know. In Peru. Our summer their winter."

She was keen to my waking confusion, the scramble of dreams and feelings in my head.

"He should have told me." I recalled the last time I saw Flaco. "We had a nice evening at Calafia. After the Tijuana bins. He had many opportunities. Maybe it's just a whim."

"People try to tell you things, Jack. They want to. It's not that you push them away. You are open to receiving *them*. But you close *yourself*. So, we become reluctant."

"That's how you feel—with me?" I asked.

"From the beginning," she replied.

"Are *you* leaving?"

"I'm here to the end." She turned to her sketch. It was Cisco. He was standing on the terra cotta walk, his broom at rest across the back of his shoulders, his wrists hooked over the handle. I had never seen him rest like that.

"Like me," I said.

She smiled, almost to a laugh, and shook her head as she looked down at her work. "See? That's what I mean. You say that. But it's a disguise. It seems like an admission. A connection. *Simpático.* But really, it's a deflection, a way of you hiding within the admission of another."

"You don't think I'm here to the end?"

She pressed the tip of her tongue to her upper lip as she brushed a delicate line of charcoal, adding a touch of sway to Cisco's stance.

"I don't think you're as certain as I am. As doomed as I am."

"You feel doomed?"

"Yes," she replied. "But not in such a bad way. It's probably best to be doomed to something than to be left floundering. All the heroes and gods end up doomed. In some kind of repetition. Constellations travelling the same path across the sky, pushing a stone, an echo."

She had other works fanned above her present sketch. One was a side view of Valeria reading as she sat atop a rock. The edge of a tree trunk framed one side, the other side open, pulling vision toward the book. Valeria held the book in an impossibly romantic manner, at arm's length, thumb crooked in the crease. What would have been the rounded parts of her—chin, shoulders, knees—were cast slightly angular.

There we were, four librarians, two real, two on paper. One was drawing, rendering two of the others, one was sweeping, one was reading. And what was I doing?

What options do we have? To keep storing books in the infinite annex, until all abandoned buildings and salt mines are filled, until we are smothered in unrequested paper? And what if Tolan's Theory of Erasure was valid? What if everything written—whether on paper or screen—was erasure? What if all annexes—digital or physical—were the detritus of that erasure, the pilings that form on the edges of rubbed out ink? I can burn a 1958 volume on volcanoes, a book treasured in its time, and no one would ever know it existed, its unique 1958 take on magma and plate tectonics lost forever. The last person to see it would be me, its destroyer.

There is a Baja legend about the grays. It's told as a children's story. Long ago, before books existed, a deal between humans and whales was struck on the shores of Scammon's Lagoon. Humans got the land, whales got the sea. As a result, whales lost their hands, their thumbs and fingers fusing into fins best adapted to water. They lost the ability to make things, to build cities, to make books and have libraries. All knowledge would have to exist and develop in verbal and physical exchange, contained in song, dance and spoken tales. Thus, their language evolved into something much vaster than ours, something that could contain and transmit whole libraries in a brief undulation of sound, something that could reach whole populations at once, across a thousand miles of ocean. A single whale would be all whales, all reading and filtering together. A single person would be just that. An individual. A single reader.

I studied Cat's sketch of Valeria. It made me think of *Alice's Adventures in Wonderland*, the drawings I had seen in an early edition, Alice's sister sitting brook-side, reading to her charge. "You could put a rabbit there," I told Cat as I pointed to the space beside Valeria's extended sandal.

"That's not what I'm after," she replied.

In order to gain perspective, I turned the sketch. Beneath was another drawing. When I slid the sketch of Valeria to the side, I unveiled a scene that filled an entire page. It disoriented me. It was a sailboat knifing through a rough sea marked by whitecaps. The boat was surrounded by waterspouts, some thin, a few thick and dark. The boat was the size of my thumb. On it, the ferryman steered the wheel while Equisa stood watch near the bow.

The figures were too small to be detailed, but you could tell one was a man and one was a woman. On the horizon, visible between waterspouts, were the distant silhouettes of the pursuing sailboats. They looked like dragonflies touching water.

I could tell what Catalina was after in this one. It reminded me of nineteenth-century adventure book drawings, the type seen in the serials of the same era, where the angles of the hands and head had to carry the sense of fear, wonder, surprise. I had no idea Catalina had been reading the novel, too.

Then I recalled that she never used bookmarks. She was one of those proud readers who didn't need them, who simply remembered the scene and closed the book. I first discovered this about Catalina during that time at Michigan, when we read together at the Landmark Library. So, I had miscounted the bookmarks in *Equisa*. There was my earmark, Valeria's paper scrap, Marisa's feather, and Catalina's memory, an invisible place unknown to the rest, evident only in what she conveyed to others.

"How far have you gotten?" I asked as I viewed the waterspouts.

"A bit past that." Catalina continued to work on the rendition of Cisco, giving me just one side glance. "She's reached Baja."

I retrieved *Equisa* from the bed and returned to the conservation room, pouring more coffee for Catalina and myself.

At one end of the stand-up desk, giving Cat the room she needed, I sipped from my mug and paged through the book. I had no focus, flipping here and there the way we often read with morning coffee.

I could have been her subject, posing at the desk, appearing thoughtful. But all I was doing was measuring the race of bookmarks. My dog ear, Valeria's torn scrap, Marisa's feather, Catalina's memory. And maybe Cisco, too. He always marked his place by noting the page number as he closed the book, a more precise and refined version of Cat's method.

The sound of Catalina's sketching grazed pleasantly along my nape, the advance of scissors through hair, more inside than outside. Did how we mark our places define us? A person who didn't know was a person who didn't read. And people who couldn't bother with a mark, who placed the book face down or dog-eared, were those who couldn't quite admit to themselves that they were truly reading, couldn't commit to the thoughts and imagination of another. They risked damaging the book for the sake of autonomy. Someone who used paper—a scrap or a dedicated bookmark—was more invested, or at least wanted to be. Someone who used a found object vaguely related to the book's subject—a feather or leaf—was giving herself over to the book, letting it or wanting it to shape her current decisions and actions.

Then what were Catalina and Cisco? Did they consider the process of reading so delicate and precise that it should not be altered by the mere presence of an object or crease across the plane? Were they utterly confident of the book's impression or of their own comprehension? Unlike those who preferred a physical mark, were they less afraid of inadvertently reading over what they had already seen, thereby re-shaping the narrative?

How perverse would it have been to re-order these marks in *Equisa*, including my own?

"Read some aloud," said Catalina. She continued to draw.

"What?"

"Where she reaches Guadalupe Valley." She concentrated on her charcoal strokes as she spoke, rendering Cisco at rest with his broom. That fascinated me. At once, she could focus on two distinct works and still consider me, us, in this moment.

"Just past where you've reached," she continued. "Her family has a vineyard there. She seeks refuge among the grapes and cousins. She cobbles together a makeshift lab in one of the cellars, using wine-making things. Read. Just a little."

I fumbled forward through the pages, skimming dialog, jumping exposition. I found a moment where Equisa finally examines the *u-r-e* corner, gives it the time. I started to read where she holds the scrap with tweezers and raises it to the light.

"Wait," said Cat. "Read that, but first go back to where she lifts the grapes."

I retraced pages, a little panicked, the way you might feel during a test you hadn't studied for.

"The last paragraph of the previous chapter." Cat swept two long charcoal lines, angled her neck for perspective.

I found the paragraph and read it. It was brief:

> On her way to the cellar lab, Equisa walks between the vines. It is just after sunrise and the light is at a low slant, shadows long and heavy, almost enough to feel. She stops to heft a ripe cluster of grapes, and without detaching the bunch from the vine, she lifts the fruit to the morning sun. All she knows is that although they are red, they will be

pressed for white wine. Against the sun, they go translucent and refract the light into sparkling points. She sees the hidden glass of white.

From this, I returned to the moment where she examines the corner scrap in her lab. All the while I wondered at Catalina's ability to know these places, to have these places marked, to conjure them even as she sketched a portrait of a colleague she has known for twenty years.

And as I read I began to fear that finishing this story, that passing all these bookmarks, visible and invisible, would propel me into loneliness, past Flaco and his promise of new friendship, past Valeria and her promise of a new librarian—past Marisa. Adrift in the solitude of the EPL with Cisco and Cat.

In the barn above the cellar, two cousins read. They sit on half-barrels which have been shaped into benches. They do not look up as they sip their book tea and scan their placards, close their eyes to the effects of the infusion, return to scanning, close their eyes. Curious, Equisa steps between them and tries to figure what they have chosen for their early morning read. One placard depicts a fat, dilapidated windmill. Too easy, she thinks.

Hoping for something more challenging, she turns to the other placard. A sparrow flies into the barn, flits among the rafters. The placard shows a speckled snake and she does have to think a moment before she knows the cousin is reading *The Adventures of Sherlock Holmes*. The sparrow dips low, its wings thrum between the three cousins and they all look up and then eye one another.

When the two see Equisa, recognize her, they close their books.

The Quixote one, a young woman asks. Have you read mine? I mean in the old way?

Five times, replies Equisa. Some parts, like those windmills, more times than that.

You could do that, says the other one, Holmes. With the old way. You could read parts over and over without paying extra. Over and over, picturing it different. Until you know it.

Sometimes by heart, says Equisa. She smiles at the way he kind of looks like Holmes. Or does she imagine that?

They say you have a piece of one with you, Quixote tells her. They tell us you plan to go get the rest. At the border.

Equisa only brushes her finger along the closed placards, tracing the image of a knight's helmet, then tapping the mug to make the tea surface ripple.

Some of us are practicing, says Holmes. To help you.

Help me?

Guard you, he answers. Protect.

Catalina, knowing the words, read out loud with me these last three lines.

Thirty-three

I WENT TO BRIGADOONS plenty early enough to catch the morning glass and the best riders. I had it in my mind to talk to Flaco, to listen to his plans about Peru, to thank him again for taking me to the Tijuana bins. He was gone.

I didn't have to check the lineup, scan the dark figures bobbing over the swells or slashing the mirrored water beneath the curl. Flaco had left five boards propped against the cliff side. Tails dug into the sand, they leaned this way and that like tombstones. The first four, sleek and modern, wax-free, were labeled with sticky notes. Each note bore nothing more than initials indicating who was to inherit the board. The fifth was a longboard, cream with three black stripes running the center of its length. Carved into the sandy wax were the letters *U R E.*

I had to climb back up the cliff and trot along the highway shoulder to get my full wetsuit. By the time I returned to the sand I was already winded. No one else was ashore. They were all out there catching waves too young for me.

I leashed my ankle to the old board and slid into the breakwater. The rollers tugged the board toward shore as the cold foam rinsed over me. Flaco said that you had to commit to a second skin if you wanted your wetsuit to work. He said it had to be how a snake felt, how you were never really warm, your blood and skin cool but alive and quivering.

Some of those in the lineup watched me get the longboard out to the swells. The short razor sticks they used now were easy in the get-out. They could nose them beneath the waves, slide forward in the quiet of the underbelly. With Flaco's old longboard, I had to take plenty of hits and tumbles as I jumped and plowed my way through the breakers. I could have hop-scotched my way along the point and slid behind the swells, but I figured this was what Flaco had pictured.

In the lineup, they turned their backs to me. I raised a finger to tell them all I wanted was just one—one ride, one simple glide and pop-up on this board trusted to me. One from the center of the lineup made his way toward me. The others parted for him. When he neared, I saw why. Villaran drew next to me.

"Why aren't you in Peru?" I asked in Spanish.

"I go tomorrow." Water dripped from his beard.

"Did you see Flaco?"

He nodded. "With those boards. Before the sun. I asked him if he wanted to ride one more."

"You'll be riding with him soon enough, no?"

Villaran eyed the horizon, letting the swell raise his view. He spoke while gazing out to sea.

"Don't try it," he said. "Paddle that thing around the point and take something smaller. Those waves will be plenty good."

"How old are you?" I asked.

"Thirty-two."

"I know why I'm out here," I said. "But why are you? You should be down there already, no? Point Panic or somewhere. Where you're tested."

"The water is too crowded at breaks like that. I like this coast. One place vanishes while another appears."

"But imagine that," I said. "As your home."

"They're skidding a little at the top," he said before paddling back to his place. "And there's a hidden step after the first drop."

The best part of a book is just before the end, when it is

still full of wonder but shed of its story. The best part of a wave is just before the drop, when you see into the future but it is all uncertain because it comes at you at breakneck speed, faster than your vision can assess. As you begin, it's like you are a split second ahead of your physical self.

I took a wave that Villaran could ride in his sleep. I anticipated the skid at the top, feeling the lip begin to curl. The face rising up beneath my board appeared bottomless, the entire cliff side reflected in its concave mirror, the rising sun there, too.

My hope was to survive the drop and I did. I got my right rail going and sliced across the face. As Villaran had warned, there was a hidden step, a wave within the wave. I fell. I was good at falling. Flaco said you have a choice and no time to make it. You either try to dig your rail in to make a save, or you bail. Hesitation gets you hurt. If you bail, fall completely and let the wave throw you. Take a big breath and give yourself to Poseidon.

The break drove me to the bottom. Eyes closed, breath held, I plowed into the sand. The turbulence above me felt as though it would go on forever, dragging me beneath it. I could not fight it, could not try to climb my way to the surface.

Flaco must have been laughing. At the bottom of the sea, I vowed to write him and tell him about this particular ride, about Villaran and what he said. Maybe I would exaggerate things. I would ask him about Peru and his local library. I wondered how far he had made it through *Equisa*. How valid were our underwater resolutions?

Flaco's board, snagged by the wave, leashed to my ankle, yanked me hard toward shore, skimming us to the surface. I let it all happen to me.

Thirty-four

MARISA AND I TRIED to meet during my noon break. I had asked and she agreed to come to the EPL. Fifteen minutes before our scheduled time, she cancelled by text. Because she offered no reason and did not call, I knew that Jimbo had somehow complicated things. Younger, I would not have understood, might not have resigned myself to the hurt, asked impossible questions, made inconsiderate demands. At fifty-one, I understood. But that understanding amplified the hurt—for her, too, I believed. True understanding is so often painful and prolonged, unrecognized. Any external expression must be kind yet genuine, independent of any internal burn, searing as that could be.

There were so many better places I would have preferred to meet. We could have camped one last time on the stark shore of Scammon's Lagoon, letting the quiet skim of ocean into desert fill our pauses, the occasional huff of a gray whale laugh away heartache. Dodging hummingbirds, we could have hiked in the wildflowers between the ruins of Tzintzuntzan. Beneath the looming Juan O'Gorman mural, we could have conversed in the Pátzcuaro library until finally hushed by the librarian before we finished all there was to say.

We had been in love with one another for over twenty-five years. Requesting any of those settings would have been reasonable—not practical, but emotionally understandable.

•

THAT EVENING I WENT to Calafia. The place closed at different times, according to the flow of the tides and highway traffic. High tide usually took out at least the three lowest levels, the mist of the waves dowsing the torches and wetting the tables and chairs. I showed up at the tide's zenith.

For cover, I carried *Equisa*. I expected to speak to Jimbo, to request a brief chat with Marisa and had a vague plan to make it about the book. I wore my shirt and tie from work, even thought about wearing my nametag.

When I arrived, three waitresses were closing up the top level. Two were flipping chairs, one was tidying the bar. The one behind the bar took one look at me and said she would go get Marisa. The other two gave me side glances as they continued their work. I stood, hands in pockets, *Equisa* wedged in the crook of my wrist, and I listened to the waves of high tide, the splat of collapsing sea geysers.

Marisa arrived. She wore a dark blue dress and carried the candle snuff. She smiled thanks at the waitress. She held the smile for me.

"Come, Jack." She raised the snuff. "Let's go do the candles."

•

SHE LED US DOWN to the fourth level. Surf spray had smothered the lower flats. Walking along the rim, I capped three of the torches. She waited for me beneath the last one, stopped my arm as I reached to cover the flame. We put our hands on each other's shoulders and pressed our foreheads together.

"If Jimbo had seen you up there," she said, "he would know everything."

"But I'm dressed as a librarian."

"It's a poor disguise."

"You expected me? Those waitresses?"

"My sentries," she said. "I had an inkling."

Our closeness—our faces so near, our crowns together—prevented us from seeing one another's expression. But I could feel the brush of her lashes, her breath on my lips and throat. We stood this way without talking. A dozen waves crashed and receded. I didn't want to speak because that would begin the end.

"There are so many places for us," I whispered. "For us to do this better."

"I know, Jack. I know those places. I will always know those places."

She took a deep breath and pulled me into an embrace, her face against my neck. I dropped the book and wrapped my arms around her back. Again, we remained quiet, counted the waves. I could feel her eyes close. I saw the night grays of Scammon's Lagoon. She saw the bright swaths of the O'Gorman mural.

When we released, I knelt to pick up *Equisa*. Marisa laughed softly at the book.

"I like her world," she said. "I know I'm not supposed to, but I do."

•

WE ASCENDED THE STAIRCASES, covering the torches on the landings, snuffing the candles embedded in the cliff walls. She climbed one step above. I took care of the candles too high for her to reach. As we progressed, the dark blue sway of her waist was level to my eyes. That night, alone in the basement bed of the EPL, I dreamed that I could breathe underwater.

Thirty-five

I WOKE WHILE IT was still dark, too dark to go to Brigadoons or do much of anything. My blood too charged to find sleep again, I read. When Equisa left the readers in the barn and went to her makeshift lab in the cellar, I discovered her plan to make a replica of the torn *u-r-e* corner.

> Using the tip of a grape leaf, Equisa creates a mock version of the torn corner. She finds the leaf in the duff beneath the vines. It is covered in the same white dust that clouds the grapes, composed of the self-protective wax generated by the vines plus traces of airborne yeasts. This will serve as her paper.
>
> To replicate ink, she uses blood and metal. To get the blood, she pricks her forearm, knowing she will need her fingers to be at their best. She needs no more than two drops and gathers these in a wine spoon, what her cousins call a *tastevin*. Into this she rasps metal powder from the blade of a hoe. The resulting liquid is still red, but she anticipates that the tannins in the dried leaf will darken the mixture to near-black. She needs the hue of the letters to have complexity, to appear *made*. She raises the leaf corner into the slant of sun coming through the high cellar window. The veins, obscured by the white patina, show through in the light. Perhaps they will mistake them, she thinks, for production flaws, for weaknesses inherent to inscribing truth on ephemeral paper.
>
> She employs the tip of an antique pen, the same pen whose hollow tube she used to breathe from beneath

the sand. The tastevin holding the blood-metal ink quivers in her left hand. Her right, positioning the pen, remains steady. She is able to inscribe the letters without looking at the original. Her strokes mimic the font and she relishes this act of penmanship, thought to surface, surface to thought. She almost feels able to write the entire book. The leaf drinks the ink. The tannins mix with her blood and metal. She encases the forgery between two shards of glass and disguises this within a necklace.

Her Guadalupe Valley cousins serve her dinner beneath the stars and beg her not to go to San Ysidro, not to try to find the rest there in the yellow house on Vidrio Street. There is no way it will still be there, they say. There is no way that anything will be there. On the border like that.

But she has to go, she tells them. Even though she sensed, upon the coyote's death, that the fragment was all that remained, she needs to see the end. Otherwise she will forever have dreams about it in various renditions. And seeing the end will help her reconstruct the entire book.

Can you really do that? they ask as they pour the best wine.

Yes, she tells them. When I get it back to the UNAM lab. Back to Murrieta Tolan.

So, they help her. Two of them travel ahead in order to flank her arrival. One travels behind. Equisa wears the forgery necklace and leaves the genuine paper fragment at the vineyard, hidden within the pinch of a wooden barrel clamp. These wine-making cousins are the most resourceful of people. They work their own vineyards, assess the grapes, man the presses, cask and bottle, distribute and sell. They cooper their own barrels. When forced, they protect their vineyards and cellars.

The yellow house on Vidrio Street is half-gone when Equisa arrives. Its chimney still stands, with two stucco walls tapering down from it. In the mounds of rubble are the splintered remains of wooden bookshelves. All of San Ysidro is a moonscape, low circles of ruin overlapping one another, gray even in this noon light. The borderline is sharp and neat, Tijuana thriving beyond with its quarry grinding in the unseen distance, the ocean to the west.

The attack on Equisa is swift. Like spiders, they pop from trap doors in the gray dust. There are five of them. As before in the Chihuahuan desert, they bind and strip her. Her hair has not grown back enough for shearing, but they comb through what's there. They yank the necklace from her throat and find the forgery. They believe it might be genuine but are not entirely convinced.

All the while, her cousins, her protectors, are absent. Why aren't they helping her? Where are they? She fears they are either killed or corrupted. But then she sees. They wait until her captors believe they are victorious, relaxed in their crime and sin, contemplating their captor's execution. The cousins approach from three different directions, a collapsing equilateral triangle. She recognizes one of them, Quixote, the woman who reads in the barn. Their pace is neither fast nor slow but is deliberate, the direction unwavering. Their targets are drunk with false victory, their center on the replica held by their leader.

Using rebar gleaned from surrounding rubble, the cousins impale three of the soldiers. This leaves the leader and her one remaining guard outnumbered and they run, Equisa's clothes and necklace in-hand.

As before in Chihuahua, Equisa cannot bring herself to wear her attackers' clothes. So, Quixote, the one closest to her size, offers hers and dons the blood-stained shirt and pants. Together, they all journey back to Guadalupe Valley, this time using a western route along the Pacific shore of Baja. They stop once to bathe in the cold ocean. Equisa uses a large stone to bring herself to the sea bottom where she walks along the sand, eyes open like an ocean-dweller, stingrays at her feet.

Using the harvest of the vineyards, her cousins throw her a farewell dinner. It is outside on a long table among the vines, lights strung overhead, a soft breeze rattling the leaves. In the coin pocket of her jeans resides the paper fragment, the three remaining letters of *The Last Cronopio.*

When I read this scene about the party, I stopped thinking so much of Marisa and instead pictured Cisco. I imagined him both young and old, hiking a stretch of rugged Baja shoreline in his newly soled leather boots, then sitting on his porch overlooking the bay, chips and lime and beer at his ready.

Thirty-five

DURING THE AFTERNOON POOL, Valeria helped man the circle. She muted the phone and wore the headset in such a way that made it appear part of her hairdo, a thin barrette extending from the sweep along the line of her jaw. You had to focus to notice she was taking calls, fielding questions only librarians could answer. Her fingers entered data on our digital holdings. Beside her keyboard stood a stack of ten from her assessment carton. When one stack was finished, she would reach into the depths of her carton and neatly pile another ten.

At once, she could talk to a caller, answer *What is the world's oldest living fossil?* and lean into her carton to fish out the titles. Her inflection would not change even as she bent at the waist, her responses smooth and assured.

"Until recently, it was the coelacanth, a deep-sea fish in the west Indian Ocean. It's been around for 360 million years." She leaned into her carton, shoulders deep, but kept answering. "But researchers discovered a species of nautilus, *Allonautilus scrobiculatus*, that has been around for 500 million years."

She smiled at whatever the caller said, squared her fresh stack of ten. "Yes," she replied. "One of those shell things we often see in rocks. Their shells actually form a logarithmic spiral."

She laughed at the response. "Yes, I guess you could say that. Math pre-dates people."

As she took calls, keyboarded and coded, checked out books for patrons, thanked returns as they came in, she found moments to assess her stack. Without turning away from her work, she would reach for the top title the way one mindlessly plucks a potato chip from a bowl. Only after she held it for a moment, wedged her thumb into the gutter, would she read. It looked as though she were performing a card trick, weighing the deck before her guess. She would peruse the front matter, sniff the gutter, then sample five random pages. Every book went down the burn chute.

This she would perform as a kind of reversal to the selection, looking at her work—her screen or a patron—while she slipped the title beneath the flap. Throughout, she kept her chin raised, shoulders and back straight.

Could any of the patrons tell that we had burned hundreds of titles just a few hours earlier? Could they smell it on us? See some sign of aftermath in our eyes? Guilt, sadness, hope, lust?

•

AMID THE CIRCLE SAT *Equisa.* Valeria's bookmark had advanced. I tried to catch up by reading right there beside her, exposed.

> Alone again, Equisa travels the length of Baja then takes a ferry off the tip to reach the mainland. She watches and hopes for waterspouts, but the sea and sky remain clear. There are other passengers on the ferry and she wonders what secrets they carry. She recalls the ferryman who took her across The Sea of Cortez and sends him good wishes, that his sails are as full as the ones above her now.
>
> She makes it back to Popocatepetl, to Murrieta Tolan's lab. She shows the scrap to her mentor. Wordlessly, Tolan eyes it, reads it over and over. She gives Equisa private lab space, warns her to keep her work secret, to establish a cover project that will hide her real work. Drawn from

behind one of her secret panels, Tolan gives her a blank book, a palimpsest she has preserved over the years for just this opportunity.

It was an encyclopedia of cocktails, Tolan explains. A bartender gave it to me thirty years ago. I erased it using condensed light, two pages at time, exposed for seven days. The *scripto inferior* is, I admit, interesting—better than most. But go ahead, she insists. Restore the erasure. Letter by letter. Word by word. Sentence by sentence. Page by page.

Equisa stares at the palimpsest. Nothing that happened before on her journey frightens her more than this. She feels her eyes widen.

You must have known, Tolan says. Soon after obtaining that corner. What you would have to do.

It wasn't knowing what I would have to do that crippled me, replies Equisa. It was knowing that I *could* do it.

I returned the book to its place between us and Valeria poked it. She removed her headset and shook her hair free, the short cut rearranging itself in vague spirals. She opened *Equisa* at my new earmark, scanned the page, then closed the book, pushing it closer to the burn flap. She spoke of the section just behind my mark.

"When you think about it," she said. "A recipe offers the best example of Tolan's Theory of Erasure." She explained that a good recipe—food or cocktails—begins and develops as something entirely oral, remembered, forgotten, tested, re-remembered. As soon as it is written down, codified, it begins to stagnate, die. The farther away it gets from the collective memory that used it, the more it embraces its written form, the less authentic it becomes.

"Do you think," she asked, "that Murrieta chose that particular palimpsest on purpose? And what happens when you erase an erasure?"

A light on the phone indicated an incoming call and I nodded to it. She just watched it flash. We both watched it until the caller was sent to hold. This activated the message light, pulsing green.

"Don't worry," she said. "I know it's just a story, not a real theory. Something D'Acquisto made up."

"But still," I replied. "He imagined it."

I slipped *Equisa* into the burn slot. We listened to the hiss of its slide, the silence of its release, the thump of its landing.

"How many times have you done that?" she asked, putting on her headset. "And are you okay with my mark ending up ahead of yours?"

•

DURING MY BRIEF LATE afternoon break, I fished *Equisa* from the bin. The basement was filled with ochre light, cut by shadows. It wasn't that I needed to be ahead of the other readers. It was even less rational than that. It was that I had fooled myself into believing that when these bookmarks passed my dog ear, then vanished beyond the last pages, so too would their bearers.

I sat on the end of the bed and read in the fading light.

> Before Equisa attaches the corner to the palimpsest, she and Tolan run a series of tests on the paper and ink. Using just one fiber, they date and qualify the stock. Equisa, whose hands are steadier than Tolan's, extracts the fiber from the tip of the corner, far from any ink. The strand reminds them of an eyelash, the way it changes in the light, disappears and reappears as Equisa turns it. They suspect

from the age and the high grade that it is probably from a major publisher and from the font they know for certain it is a novel. The late return to ink, after decades of laser, supports all of these notions. Somewhat in jest, the two of them begin to refer to the project as *The Last Cronopio*.

Tolan excuses herself from the lab, claims she has an important meeting with a visiting archivist. But Equisa knows she is removing her presence, assuring optimal focus for the close work. Equisa is still not comfortable being alone with the corner scrap even though she has traveled with it over entire deserts, seas, and peninsulas.

She uses a microscope to examine the letters. She has been dreaming of this moment and fearing it. The scope's view appears on an overhead screen that looms in blackness. The letters are the size of her head. The ink, thick as tar, undulates and skips over the fibers.

The suffix *–ure* creates an abstract noun of action. It originates from Old French and Latin. At the time of this text's publication, ninety-four words ended in *ure*.

Equisa slides the view toward the torn edge of the corner, where the word has been peeled. Here the paper becomes thinner before it ends in a feathery weave of singular fibers. In the light of the scope and the amplification of the overhead screen, the white is translucent. Specks of ink cling to the fibers.

In the luminescent plane preceding the *u*, she connects the dots into an *n*, the *u* inverted. She runs through the dictionary in her head. *Tenure and manure*. She smiles as though recognizing a song. She increases the magnification and begins tracing single fibers that finger their way into the abyss. She searches for the smallest bit of ink, even a dark shade spot left by a fallen speck, even an indentation along a fiber where heavy liquid had dried and torn away the surface.

She locates a vertical series of four. She imagines the Galilean moons, how they line up perfectly against Jupiter's mass of colors, three dots close together, one away. The letter *i*.

Inure. She has the word. She feels it. She removes the corner from beneath the scope and reads. She reads the word in its entirety. Its meaning slams into her. Its idiosyncrasies and implications charge her nerves. She needs to attach the corner to a page, where the letters can begin to expand into text. It is an unusual enough word, especially as it is here, used in either present or future tense. It is highly active. *Inure*.

She hurries to show Murrieta Tolan.

I felt light-headed. The book lay closed in my lap as I sat on the edge of the basement bed. Instead of pressing down on me, the whole of the library above seemed to tug me upward, into the rise of its stacks. Vertigo is common among librarians, even those working in small, one-room buildings. The head librarian in Oban moved there from Glasgow for a cure but going from large to small didn't end her dizzy spells. Though theories abound—a task that involves myriad head positions, many sudden shifts between close, middle, and distant vision—the reason remains a mystery.

I considered what it might be like to be cursed with Equisa's reading ability. I thought of venturing into the stacks three floors above, standing in the slant of near-evening light, and selecting a book to read. Would I be able to read the last word of a chapter and know what came before? It felt possible. If almost all access to books were removed, it felt likely.

I fantasized myself as savant, peering at the torn corner as it loomed on the microscope screen. My vertigo increased. The room spun until I felt as though on the other end of the scope, the subject being read. I shivered, let the dizziness subside. Footsteps along the main floor overhead stirred then steadied my thoughts, called me back to work. I folded a new earmark, pages ahead of the slip and the feather.

Thirty-six

I RETURNED THAT NIGHT, hours after closing, to burn 800 more books with Catalina. Into Cuervo's fire we would heave titles sent by San Diego, Los Angeles, and San Francisco. We would question nothing, averting our gaze from volumes that were clearly not assessments, that bore silver Deweys on their spines—that *felt* like books that had been read for years.

As usual, I entered through the basement access and wandered the dimness of the loading bay, the conservation room, the studio while waiting for Catalina to appear, ghost-like, from wherever she gathered her cartons. A sleeping figure on the studio bed prompted another spell of vertigo. It was a woman, curled on her side, atop the covers, a book splayed beneath a reaching hand. In the gray light I had to move close to see if it was Catalina, Marisa, or Valeria. Her dress was tucked neatly about her knees, her feet bare. No light was on. She must have fallen asleep while the evening glow was enough for reading. I recalled those days, when I would read like that, into the fading light, entranced, outside time, unwilling to cut the atmosphere that had gathered with the blend of book and world.

Given the vertigo I was fighting, it could have been Equisa, taking a rest from her work in the lab. But it was Valeria. Maybe she suspected what Cat and I had been doing and hoped to catch us in the act. She was too young to spend the night in a library.

I used a lighter from one of Cat's nearby stashes to illuminate more, trusting the soft glow wouldn't waken Valeria. Her lips were parted, breath soft and rhythmic. Her eyelids quivered in REM. I knew the book before I held the flame to its cover.

Only for a moment did I feel intrusive. She was the one who said this was a public library, not a house. And it was likely she had already done the same with me. How had I appeared under the flame? Did my lashes flutter as I dreamed? Was the book beyond my grasp? Was Marisa in my arms?

I slid *Equisa* from beneath her fingers, inserted Valeria's bookmark into place, secured Marisa's feather and, using both hands, pressed the novel closed for the last time, the way we do when we finish a good read, perhaps hold it to our chest for a moment.

When I reached the doorway, Catalina was there, watching. She placed a hand to my shoulder and nodded toward the sleeping Valeria.

"Our bastard child," she whispered. "What have we spawned here? A race of super-readers who relish the scent of scorched paper?"

"I think she might leave," I said.

"Even if she does," she replied, "this place has changed her."

Moving expertly in the dark, Catalina found a blanket from the closet and placed it gently over Valeria, tucked it along her spine, tapered it beneath her chin. I drew a glass of water and set it on the nightstand. On his outcrop up the hillside, Cuervo groaned and creaked as the fire inside him expanded his metal form, lifted his wings closer to the stars.

•

EQUISA RODE WITH US as we towed that night's 800 books to the incinerator. As she drove, Catalina would occasionally glance down at the book riding between us, then look at me. Years back, the New York City Public Library abandoned its plans to renovate its main branch on Fifth Avenue. The renovation centered on the removal of five floors of stacks, annexing millions of books in New Jersey storage, to make room for readers and to emphasize lending over holdings. The renovation was halted due to a city-wide grassroots movement based largely on sentiment. A love of books.

But also, Cat and I believe, a distrust of books. Of what value is a 1958 book on volcanoes? Whatever worthwhile knowledge it contained has been absorbed and extended by later editions. Maybe it had quaint drawings and other graphics. But as librarians—Baja librarians—we believe the space that book takes up is more valuable than the book itself. We trust and have hope that people will do better, learn, read, continue to fill that space while creating another.

We loved readers. Sometimes together, most times apart, we traveled the world to see other libraries.

For the third time, Catalina checked *Equisa* then me.

"When is the next good conference?" I asked.

She maneuvered the cart and trailer around a dark bend, barely grazing the walls of scrub oak. Keeping her eyes on the moonlit path ahead, her arm locked to the wheel, she rubbed her chin against her bicep.

"There's one this summer," she answered, eyes ahead. "Peru. In Trujillo."

"We should go."

"It will be winter there."

"I'll pack my wetsuit. One for you, if you want to finally learn. Besides, it's never winter or summer there, right? *La capital de la primavera eternal.*"

"Everlasting anything sounds like hell to me," she replied. "Spring or otherwise. But sure. I'll claim our spot at the conference."

•

Before we set about the burning, Catalina walked to the edge of the outcrop. She hugged herself as she stared into the darkness, gripped her shoulders as though she were cold. With nothing to do, on the verge of feeling excluded, I joined her. Cuervo's fire burned white hot behind us, the press of light making the world beyond the edge darker. The lights of Ensenada looked like the deep and broken bottom of a vast cave dusted with luminescent mineral.

I wrapped my arms about her, more for myself than for her. She rested her head back against my chest and I feared she could sense the beat of my heart.

"Don't ever get used to this," she said. "Don't ever let me get used to it."

We opened the first carton and tossed the first armfuls into Cuervo's belly, she first, I following in rhythm to her sway. She had learned to fill and order the boxes according to their incendiary quality, starting with volumes brittle as kindling, stoking Cuervo. These would be followed by the more resistant titles, thick and moldy, their pages unturned for decades. Then we would return to some of the more flammable books in order to revive the flames.

Midway, after the fourth carton, we took our usual break, stretching our backs, easing our eyes on the darkness, walking out our thoughts. I retrieved *Equisa* from the cart seat and brought it to the incinerator. Catalina finished her stretch and returned to task, cutting open the next carton. I placed *Equisa* atop the first layer.

She brushed her finger along the tips of the two bookmarks, pried her nail into my dog ear, about twenty pages from the end.

"Where are you?" I asked. "Did you finish?"

"Not quite," she replied. "But Cisco did. If I need, I'll ask him."

"Or we could figure it out together."

She lifted *Equisa* and handed it to me. "It's your assessment. Your honors."

During the break, Cuervo's flames had subsided. But the embers, composed of the heat-encrusted ashes of thousands of volumes, glowed a coppery green, made a wanting, hissing sound. I looked once more to Catalina as I received the book. Her expression was sympathetic, her eyes steady to mine. Maybe she knew why. Like her, I did not ever want to become accustomed to this. To enjoy it at times, to need it for release and reminder, would be acceptable. But, though we often chucked volumes in by the armload, we wanted it to feel as though we were disintegrating every sentence, sentences we had to deny ourselves.

The titles we were burning at night were books. They were not assessments, aspirants, pretenders. Despite our deliberate comportment, our self-imposed blinders, our librarian eyes and arms told us these books were getting better. Somewhere ahead would we then cross a line, begin worldwide destruction from this odd splinter of land? Or would we begin a reversal?

A cloud of bats passed through our light, feeding on moths drawn to the flame. Their sound was wet and metallic, a thousand tiny gears squeaking. We have two very old books in the EPL that describe how moths and bats come from the moon, travel its beams to the night side of our planet. Oddly, they are in the 527s of the Dewey Decimal System, celestial navigation.

As though enjoying the air, Catalina lifted her arms to the swarm. I let her enjoy the moment, let the air clear overhead, then tossed Equisa into the flames. The palm that held the paper scrap was the last thing to disappear in the slow explosion. The fire curled the cover in such a way that made it seem as though the hand were closing over the letters.

Thirty-seven

Cisco neared the stoop with his broom. The bougainvillea on either side of the terra cotta path leaned toward one another, almost completing a crimson archway above his progress. The doors to the EPL were propped open, which meant Valeria was already at work. Inside the circle desk that day's four assessment cartons waited, initialed by Catalina. Sea air swept across the foyer, through the arch, and into the reading room where Valeria readied the tables.

She switched on a few of the lamps, one every other table, inviting readers to come sit a while with their findings. Each delicate pull of the chain resounded in the cavernous room, echoes of last words read. Equisa attaches the corner to its page, the page to its quire, the quire to its book. Cisco's broom brushed the dampened terra cotta, three whispers followed by the scrape of his bucket.

Acknowledgments

I thank Jonis Agee and Brent Spencer for supporting this work and bringing it to readers. I will always be indebted to Elise Blackwell for her life-long devotion, support and inspiration.

About the Author

A native of southern California, DAVID BAJO is the author of three previous novels: *The 351 Books of Irma Arcuri*, *Panopticon*, and *Mercy 6*. He holds an MFA from UC-Irvine and is a professor at the University of South Carolina, where he directs the MFA program in creative writing. Wherever and whenever he travels, he makes sure to visit the libraries, small as well as grand, empty or brimming, quiet or loud. Tiny local ones, especially those with ocean views, are his favorites. The Ensenada Public Library is the 2017 winner of the Brighthorse Prize for the Novel.

CPSIA information can be obtained
at www.ICGtesting.com
Printed in the USA
BVHW03s1454120918
527281BV00006B/443/P